"No! You cannot have my pants,"

Hal protested, determined to make his final stand. Shannon had already decimated his entire wardrobe, and he wouldn't let her take these with her. "This is my favorite pair of jeans and you're not getting them off my body."

Shannon rubbed her hands together evilly. She raised an eyebrow. "What if I made it worth your while?"

"What do you mean by that?"

"What would you like me to mean?"

Was she offering him sex if he took off his pants for her? He grew hard at the thought. "Well, a guy can always fantasize," he said before he could stop himself.

"So can a girl," she purred. "But the reality is so much more satisfying, don't you think?" Then she whipped off her top.

Dear Reader,

Have you ever despaired over something that your boyfriend was wearing? And worse, you were unable to stop him from *wearing it out of the house?*

When you subtly tried to tell him that something else might look better, he just shrugged and said he didn't care, right? Or when you told him flat out that his clothes would embarrass you, he got mad, and wore them just to spite you.

I have been in this situation many times! And of course it's led to fantasies of smoking the offending clothing on the barbecue grill, or tossing the guy's entire wardrobe into the garbage. While I've never actually done this, I decided that it was high time I wrote a character who did…and gave her justification for her actions by making them part of her job.

I hope you'll enjoy Shannon making over Hal—and the sizzling results. Making a guy "cool" has never gotten Shannon so hot!

Be sure to look for *Open Invitation?,* the next book in THE MAN-HANDLERS series, coming in October!

I love to hear from readers, so feel free to contact me at Karen@KarenKendall.com or write to me c/o Harlequin Enterprises, Ltd., 225 Duncan Mill Road, Don Mills, Ontario M3B 3K9, Canada.

Happy reading,

Karen Kendall

Books by Karen Kendall

HARLEQUIN BLAZE
195—WHO'S ON TOP?*

*The Man-Handlers

KAREN KENDALL
Unzipped?

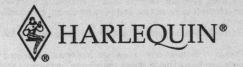

HARLEQUIN®

TORONTO • NEW YORK • LONDON
AMSTERDAM • PARIS • SYDNEY • HAMBURG
STOCKHOLM • ATHENS • TOKYO • MILAN • MADRID
PRAGUE • WARSAW • BUDAPEST • AUCKLAND

ISBN 0-373-79205-0

UNZIPPED?

1

SHANNON SHANE FIRED into her office like a bullet and ripped through her appointment book. "Oh, thank God it's tomorrow, not today." She fell into her bright yellow leather office chair, her long legs sprawled in front of her.

Jane O'Toole, her business partner, followed her in and said dryly, "Last time I checked, today really *is* today. Tomorrow never comes."

Shannon turned, pulled aside the blond curtain of hair hanging over her face and rolled her eyes at Jane. "Funny. Not. I meant my appointment with Doris Rangel. I've misplaced my Palm Pilot somewhere, and I couldn't remember. Whew. She's the new junior senator from Norwich, and we've got several wardrobe and media-training sessions set up."

Jane walked into the common area of Finesse, their business, opened the drawer of the reception desk—a somewhat useless accoutrement since they couldn't yet afford to hire a receptionist—and pulled out the missing personal organizer.

"Shan, you are no longer allowed to put anything down while you set the office alarm. It never makes it out the door with you, whether it's sunglasses, keys or a Palm Pilot."

"Yeah, I know," Shannon said ruefully. "Give me that, thanks. I need to chain it to my wrist." She stuck the device on her desk and blew out a breath. "Do we have coffee?"

"Yes. Lilia made some. If you're nice to her and say please, she might give you a cup." Adorable, but excruciatingly proper Lilia London was their third business partner in Finesse, a training center for personal and career enhancement.

Jane, benign control freak that she was, excelled at the job of CEO. She also did counseling and employee management consulting. Lilia, their resident Miss Manners, handled business and social etiquette. And Shannon herself was their image consultant and media trainer.

"Hey, I'm always nice," she said. "I'm your little ray of sunshine around here."

"Well, you're definitely a breath of fresh air…" Jane's voice trailed off as she inspected Shannon's ensemble for the day: hot-pink suede pants, black spike-heeled boots and a short, black leather jacket over a lacy camisole. "Hon, you live in *Connecticut* now. You have left Rodeo Drive. It rains here, it's gray seventy percent of the time, and New Englanders *don't wear pink pants.*"

"This one does," Shannon said firmly. "It's April,

therefore it's spring. Pink is perfect for the season. And you can wear all the gray and khaki you want, but I refuse. It's boring."

Jane adopted a resigned expression as she looked beyond the tasteful reception area, furnished with antique reproductions, an oriental rug and traditional paintings, and into Shannon's office. She closed her eyes against the tangerine-colored walls, the movie posters, the strange contemporary art.

Shannon just laughed. "Image, honey. That's what I do. My image is different from yours."

"Thank you, God," muttered Jane. "At least you're no longer wearing that green nail polish."

"That might be a little too much for the average preppy to swallow," Shan agreed.

Lilia emerged from the kitchen with two cups of coffee and handed one to Shannon, having to look up as she did so. Five foot one herself, she complained, "I think you grew another inch last night. It's not fair."

"Thanks for the java," Shannon said. "And I keep telling you, being six feet tall is not that wonderful. With a pair of heels, I dwarf most men."

Lil raised an elegant, dark-winged eyebrow. "But I'd *like* to be worshipped. It must be nice."

Shannon shook her head and drained a third of her coffee in one gulp. "Stop it. Nobody worships me."

"Uh-huh." Jane's tone was sardonic. "I was out with you last weekend. I saw the men in person—at least four Worshippers From Afar, three Droolers, a couple of would-be Leg Humpers and one Pathetic Pick-up Liner."

"Oh, him." Shan shuddered. "The nice-girl-in-a-place-like-this guy. I didn't think anybody still dredged *that* line up. Horrific."

What nobody, including her closest friends, seemed to understand was that it wasn't enjoyable to be the subject of all that male attention. It was more annoying—and the guys weren't really interested in who she was, but what she looked like. Some glossy blond American ideal. However, Shannon didn't say anything. She had learned long ago that most women considered hers high-class worries. Six-foot, one-hundred-twenty-five-pound blondes never inspired much pity. Hatred, yes. Envy, certainly. But sympathy? Out of the question.

She changed the subject, embarrassed. "So I handed out over twenty business cards at the University Women's Club dinner last night."

"Good work. Now let's hope at least five percent of them call." Jane picked up the ringing phone. "Finesse, Jane O'Toole speaking."

Shannon and Lilia moved into the kitchen as she took the business call. "So how's your grandma, Lil?"

Her friend sighed. "She's...putting a brave face on things. Knee replacement surgery is just no fun, any way you look at it. It hurts her a lot. She loves the basket of teas and cookies you brought her, though."

"Well, good. Hope she's using it, not just admiring the arrangement. I'll have to go see her again later this week. Poor thing."

"She refuses to take the roses out of the china teapot, even though they're quite wilted at this point. Once I manage to toss them—probably while she's asleep—she might let me actually make tea in the pot."

Shannon laughed. "Please forbid her to write me a thank-you note."

Lil tucked her straight dark hair behind her ears. "Already done. Heavy, monogrammed, cream paper—engraved, no thermography. Written with an actual fountain pen. Wax seal. First class stamp. Most likely sitting in your mailbox this second."

Groan. "At least we know you come by your manners honestly, Miz Vanderbilt."

Lilia's expression came as close to an actual eye roll as she would ever get.

"Give Nana a real hug from me—the boob-squashing, shoulder-to-shoulder affectionate kind, okay? Not one of those air-kiss-to-dry-cheek, flutter-fingers-on-back types." Shannon mimicked a freeze-dried socialite.

"I'll do that."

"Hey, Lil? Do you know a Peggy Underwood? Small, high energy, shock of red hair?"

"Yes. Let's see, I met her through…" She pursed her lips, thinking. "Oh, at the veterinarian's. She had a cockatiel. I had Pierre, Nana's poodle, there for his shots. Anyway, we got to talking and I gave her one of your cards. She mentioned a brother who needs help."

"Yeah. A lot of help, from what she told me—she stopped by yesterday. Said I'd have to call him, since her nagging might not get good results."

"That's a little awkward, isn't it?"

"Yup. Picture me calling. 'Hello, Mr. Underwood? I hear you're looking straight off the set of *Planet of the Apes,* honey. Come see me, would ya, dear?'"

Lil choked on her coffee. "Subtle. Very subtle."

Shan took a mock bow. "My specialty."

"You don't even know how to spell subtle, darling." Lil tipped the rest of her coffee into her mouth and moved toward the pot for a refill.

"I don't want to spell it," Shannon said. "My business is to teach people how to make a statement. A powerful statement. Subtle doesn't cut it."

"Subtle can be powerful," Lil disagreed.

"No, it's *conformist.*"

"It's *confident.*"

"Color is confident. Subtle is meek."

"Not meek, elegant."

"Why, Lil! You're arguing. That's not polite." Shannon laughed as her friend's eyes snapped. "Okay, we'll call it a draw. Anyway, so what would *you* say if you had to contact this Underwood guy?"

"I'd tell him that you met his sister and that she suggested you give him a call to set up an appointment. Straightforward, true, no awkwardness about it."

Shannon nodded. "Okay. I can do that. I'll wait a couple of days to see if he gets in touch first, though.

I don't want to be pushy." She finished her own coffee and went for a second cup.

Jane, from the doorway, said, "Oh, please don't do that! You on too much caffeine is scary."

Shannon put a hand on her hip and grinned wickedly. "Hey, Jane. What happens when a psychologist and a hooker spend the night together?"

"No! Not more shrink jokes…"

"In the morning, each of them says, 'One hundred and twenty dollars, please.'" She laughed at Jane's pained expression.

"Hey, what's the difference between—"

Jane clapped her hands over her ears.

"—a psychologist and a magician?" She spoke louder. "A psychologist pulls habits out of rats!"

Her friend backed out of the kitchen. "I have work to do now. Keep your terrible jokes to yourself."

"Aw, c'mon. One more. Why is psychoanalysis so much cheaper for a man than a woman?"

"I'm *not* encouraging you."

"Because when it's time to go back to childhood, a man is already there."

"That's no joke," Jane said, with a smirk.

"Ha. See, I have wisdom to impart. You should listen to me."

"Lilia, we've gotta start making the coffee halfcaf. She's out of control again!"

Lil poked her head around the corner and narrowed her eyes. "You know…it's almost as if she's had sugar this morning."

Shan gave them a Mona Lisa smile.

"Doughnuts!" they shrieked.

She dangled her keys and Jane made a grab for them. One benefit of being tall was that keep-away was so easy. "Krispy Kremes. I left them in the car," she said. "Just to be mean."

2

"PEGGY, LEAVE ME ALONE!" Hal Underwood said to his little sister. He brushed the hair out of his eyes again and pushed up his glasses. "This company's going public in a month, and I have one or two things to take care of." *Not to mention some detective work to do...*

Peggy Underwood, five foot two, red-headed and snub-nosed, stood her ground. Under any other circumstances, she'd be adorable. Today, she was a menace.

"I will *not* leave you alone. You've been a loner all your life, and it's time for that to change. Whether you like it or not, Hal, it's not healthy for a thirty-five-year-old man to date his computer!"

Hal devoted his right brain to her, while multitasking with his left. The criticism bounced right off him. *A cow has four stomachs. If only I had four brains, I could keep up with everything.*

"Hal! Did you hear me?"

"Yes, I heard you. I am *not* romantically involved with my computer."

Peg narrowed her eyes. "Do you have dinner with it?"

Hal shrugged and nodded.

"Breakfast?"

He sighed.

"You even take it to bed, don't you?"

I'm going to lose this battle.

"You. Are. Dating. Your. Computer."

"Peggy, for chrissakes, did Mom put you up to this?" Hal cracked his neck, in hope of easing some tension. *How the hell has my company sprung an information leak?*

"No. Although yesterday, the last thing she said to me on the phone was, 'Oy, veh—I'm a cliché!'" Peggy shook her head. "As a poet, that's her worst nightmare, you know. To be a cliché. But there's no denying she wants grandchildren."

"So get on with it, Pegs." Hal ignored her for his computer screen. *Has someone hacked in?*

"Oh, no. I've told you—it's not my fate to procreate."

"Is that what you said to Mom?" *We've locked down the firewalls and secured all the servers. It can't be the e-mail system. We monitor that 24-7.*

Peggy nodded. "You know things have more impact with Mom if they rhyme."

Hal rolled his eyes. "Oy veh—ridiculous. She's not even Jewish."

"The rhyme, Hal. Her version of reason."

"Well, here's my version of reason—*go away.* I'm trying to work." He brushed the hair from his eyes a second time. It flopped back again immediately.

"Hal, have you looked into a mirror lately? You resemble a serial killer. When was the last time you got a haircut? And that shirt—has it been wadded up in a trash bag?"

"Dryer," he mumbled, his fingers flying over the keyboard of his PC.

Peggy did her best to loom over him, but she didn't cast much of a shadow. "Hal. Hal, if you don't pay attention to me this minute, I will pull out all the cords from the back of this computer. I'll count to three."

Hal didn't register the words until she got to "three" and actually laid hands on his Precious. "Step away from the computer, Peg."

"Pay attention."

"I'm warning you. Remember that time I stuffed you into the hideaway sofa? I promise you that's nothing compared to what I'll do if you pull one cord."

"Good. You're paying attention," Peg said with satisfaction.

"What?"

"Mom and I have found the perfect place for you. And by the way, Ryan agrees."

Ryan Cabela was his attorney and good friend. He sat on the board of Hal's software company. "Ryan? What's Ryan got to do with you and Mom?" *Can Ryan be the leak?* Hal pushed the thought away. *No. He's your best friend.*

"Just that we're all in agreement. You need a new image, Hal. When the company goes public, you're going to have to deal with people. And you can't look or act the way you do now."

Hal stared at her. "What's wrong with me? Jeez, I'll get a haircut. There's a barber down the street."

"Hal, honey, I don't want to hurt your feelings, but you need a bit more than a haircut. You need a whole new image and a handler. You need media training, too."

"A *handler?* Oh, thanks very much, Peg!" Hal erupted from his chair and surged around the desk. He folded his arms across his chest and glared down at her. "I handle myself just fine. I'll go see a barber, even shave off the face fuzz." He fingered the itchy growth on his chin.

Peg shook her head. "Hal. Listen to me. You look only slightly better than Saddam when he came out of his hidey-hole—"

Hal's jaw dropped. "That is *not* true."

"Maybe a slight exaggeration, but not by much."

"Would you like to check me for lice? Rat droppings?"

"Eeeuuww." Peggy wrinkled her nose. "Calm down, Hal. I'm just trying to tell you that you need a major overhaul in the grooming, fashion and conversational departments. You've got to woo the media now. And we wouldn't mind you wooing some women, either."

"What's wrong with my *conversation?*"

"You need to speak in sentences, in English, not C++. And normal people don't call their computers 'My Precious.'"

"It's a joke," Hal explained with heavy patience.
"It's *weird*."

Hal sighed. "Fine. Whatever. But I don't see why
you're so concerned about the media."

Ryan, his attorney and the neighboring office ten-
ant, stuck his head through the door. "There is a definite need to be concerned, Hal. Sorry to eavesdrop,
but it's about time we had this talk. Peg and I are per-
forming an image intervention here." He took a bite
of the ham sandwich in his right hand and pushed up
his glasses with the left.

Hal folded his arms and glared at Ryan. "Begging
your pardon, sir, I hadn't realized you were chief
counsel for *GQ*."

"What I look like doesn't matter," Ryan said.
"What *you* look like does. You are the CEO of Underwood Technologies. If you resemble a caveman,
people will assume U.T. is run by an unstable loon.
We want them to buy stock, not wonder about your
mental health."

Hal threw up his hands. "They're buying part of
the company, not part of me! And my mental health
is just fine."

"You are the face of the company, Hal. The face
and the voice—and the future. It's time for a new
image, my man."

IT'S TIME for a new image, my man. The words rever-
berated in Hal's head as he glared at the business card
in his hand. He'd finally chased off Peg and Ryan

after promising to call the number on the card. *What crap.* Hadn't he started his own company so that he could avoid such things as dress codes, brownnosing and Corporate Career Ken dolls?

Finesse, said the card. Shannon Shane, Image Consultant and Media Trainer. No doubt she'd try to dress him in khaki pants and a navy blazer, the Connecticut State Uniform. She'd try to dye his hair blond and cap his teeth. She'd chase him with a pair of penny loafers—but she'd never get him into them.

Hal wiggled his toes in his ancient running shoes with the frayed, grungy laces. *No freakin' penny loafers, by God.* He glared at the card again before picking up the phone and dialing.

"Finesse, Shannon Shane speaking."

Shannon. The only females he'd ever known named Shannon had been gorgeous and stuck-up. Like Heathers and Tiffanys.

"Hello?"

Hal cleared his throat. "Uh, hi. I'm, uh. Well, I wanted to make an appointment."

"Okay, I'd be happy to do that. Will you tell me your name?"

God, the unknown Shannon's voice was sexy. Throaty and a bit raw. "Uh, name. Right. I'm Hal. Underwood."

"Great, Hal. I think I heard that you might get in touch. You were referred by…?"

"My—uh, sister." *Could I sound more lame?* Yup.

"And my mother." *Worse and worse.* "Oh, and my attorney." *Perfect.*

A faint tremor of laughter sifted through her voice. "Sounds like they ganged up on you."

"Yeah, pretty much."

"And you don't appreciate it."

"No. Not really."

"What do they— What do you think the issue is?"

He remembered Peg's comments, and they stung. "I'm taking my software company public in a month," he said. "And apparently…" He paused. "Apparently I look worse than Saddam when they found him in the hole."

There was no mistaking her amusement this time, though she tried to pass off the gurgle as a cough. "I—I see. Sounds urgent. Why don't we make an appointment for tomorrow afternoon?"

"You work Saturdays?"

"We often do, to accommodate our clients' schedules. Is one o'clock convenient for you?"

"Fabulous. Wonderful. Couldn't be better. I will *live,*" Hal said through gritted teeth, "for one o'clock."

"If it's any comfort to you at all," Shannon Shane told him, "Saddam cleans up very well. Of course, he could do with an eye lift."

Hal stared disbelievingly at the receiver of his telephone before punching the off button. What had he just gotten himself into?

3

TODAY WAS A TYPICAL Saturday, but Shannon didn't recognize her own body. *Who is that, reflected in my glass office door? It's an Unidentified Flying Blonde, aka me, moi, myself. The same self I was yesterday, but...not.*

Adopted. She was adopted.

She hovered like an alien outside her reflection in the door of Finesse.

Her image looked back at her: a tall, rangy blonde in black leather pants, black spike-heeled boots and a cropped, orange leather jacket. But she could have been watching another person approach. Her mind, usually sharp and aware, floated above her shoulders: detached in a helium balloon and connected by only a ribbon.

And I'm not even on drugs. She felt insubstantial, as if she could simply fade through the door like a wraith. *Who is that woman entering my place of business? Who is she?*

Shannon pulled up short between the two plaster urns full of ivy that flanked the door and put out a hand to connect with the heavy steel handle. *Pull to open. Step over threshold. Smile at Jane and Lilia, your friends and business partners.*

Jane looked up from her desk and peered into the reception area. "Shannon? Are you okay?"

"Huh? Oh. Yeah."

Lilia came out of her office with her appointment book and cell phone. "You look tired. Did you sleep last night?"

"Not much," Shannon admitted.

"Out partying late?"

Shannon shook her head. She thought about lying to Jane and Lil, telling them that she'd stayed up late watching a movie or reading a book. Instead she just bypassed them and went to the kitchen for coffee. *Pull yourself together.*

She had three different appointments today, and she couldn't be in space like this. But she had a feeling that she'd never walk steadily on earth again.

Melodramatic tendencies, Shannon. You're not auditioning for daytime soaps anymore. The voice in her head sounded just like Mrs. Koogle's, their ninth-grade English teacher.

It was a shame she wasn't reading for the soaps today. Because at least in the auditions, she'd had a script to follow, lines to memorize, the anchors of the character and a plot. Plus the adrenaline of the circumstances: will this be my lucky break? Will I get a callback?

Today she had no adrenaline. No script. No

happy—or even cliff-hanger—ending. Nope, this was her life. And while there had been days when she felt it was stuck in an endless, quaint New England traffic roundabout, at least she'd been moving. Her mother's revelation yesterday had brought her to a complete standstill.

Lil followed her into the kitchen and Shannon could feel her friend's concerned gaze on her back. *If she touches me, I'm done for.*

Lil's small hand slipped between her shoulder blades and rubbed gently in a circular motion.

So much for my mascara. Shannon's eyes overflowed. Tears of shock, hurt and confusion rolled down her nose and cheeks—and would probably have ended up in her coffee mug if Lil hadn't handed her a paper towel.

"What's the matter, honey?"

Shannon blinked at her and wiped at her nose. *Useless to try to keep this inside.* "I went to dinner at Mother's yesterday."

Lil nodded.

"The typical setup. Polished silver and crisp white linen. The Duncan Phyfe table set for two. Lobster bisque and arugula salad and some fancy French wine of hers…" *Woeful sniff.* "And of course she tells me my skirt is too short and that it's trashy to expose my midriff and she practically calls the cops to remove my toe ring."

"She doesn't mean to make you feel bad," said Lil. "She's trying to protect you from other people's judgment—and there's a lot of it in Greenwich. It's not a town full of tolerance."

"I know, I know." Shannon blew her nose. "That's why I got the hell out and took off for L.A. after college. I couldn't handle Greenwich anymore. God, they sell bottled repression in the grocery, there! In your choice of flavors—wild cherry, lemon zest, or peach blossom." She shuddered.

"So you had dinner," Lil prompted.

"Yeah. And I knew there was something weird going on, because I had to ask her for some family medical history on the phone the other day. She wouldn't tell me anything, just said I should come for dinner Friday. So we're sitting there staring at each other over these piles of arugula—I hate arugula! It tastes like grass—and she drops the bomb on me. *I'm adopted.*"

"What?"

Shannon nodded her head, then shook it, and then nodded again. "Yeah. After all these years, she tells me. Says it's time that I know. I can't believe this. All these years, I've thought I was someone that I'm…not."

Lil stared at her for a long moment and then sat gracefully on one of the kitchen stools, tucking her dark hair behind her ears. "I don't know what to say."

"This one's not in Amy Vanderbilt, is it?" Shannon sniffed again and smiled blearily through her tears.

"Not exactly." Lil hopped off the stool again and moved forward with open arms to give her a hug. "I don't think I've seen you cry in years."

"Oh, trust me, I did my share in L.A.," Shannon assured her, "while I was failing miserably as an actress." Never completely comfortable with affection, she stepped quickly out of Lil's arms after a perfunctory pat. But she was grateful for the hug—even if she couldn't quite accept it.

This time, they both sat on the tall stools at the little tiled counter, Shannon gripping her mug with both hands. She gazed into it as if it were a crystal ball—one that could tell her about the past as well as the future.

"Does your mother know anything about your biological parents? Why did she wait this long to tell you? You're twenty-nine!"

Shannon shrugged. "Rebecca Shane is always an enigma. I love her, of course, but we've always been so different. I don't quite fit her specifications." She took a sip of coffee. "Apparently my father never wanted to tell me I was adopted. It didn't make any difference to him, and he thought it would just hurt me." She blew her nose again.

"Which it does…I feel like they've lied to me all these years, and it's so weird to think that the woman who gave birth to me *gave me away.* Like a puppy or something."

"Shannon, it's not the same thing at all. She was probably in difficult circumstances, and she did it out of love. Out of concern that she couldn't give you the kind of life she wanted for you."

"How do you know, Lil? It's possible that she just didn't want to be burdened by a baby."

"Nobody can know for sure except for her. But why are you automatically looking for the negative side? It's possible that she made the most unselfish, amazing choice, one that must have been incredibly difficult."

The coffee wasn't answering any of these questions. It stared back at Shannon, brown and bland and flat. She pushed it aside.

Lilia asked again, "So what does your mother know? What details did she give you?"

Shannon twisted her long curly hair into a knot and secured it with a pencil from a can on the countertop.

"She knows very little about my biological mother and father—only some basics. Apparently this woman who gave birth to me was very young, just out of high school. My bio father was a student at one of the local colleges. He played basketball for B.U. They were from completely opposite religious backgrounds—he was Catholic, she was Jewish."

"Do you want to find out more?"

Shannon fidgeted and crumpled what was left of the paper towel into a ball. "I don't know. I'm torn. For better or for worse, my parents are the people who raised me. The ones who spoon-fed me and changed my diapers and kept me from sticking my fingers into electrical outlets. The ones who taught me how to read and ride a bike. The ones who sent me to college. You know?"

Lilia nodded.

"I may never be proper enough for Rebecca, but

she's my *mom*. It's *her* voice in my head that governs my basic human values—her voice and Dad's. Not the voices of two strangers who happened to conceive me at a frat party or something."

"But you can't help wondering."

"No. I am so utterly confused and blindsided by this—" Shannon checked her watch "—and I need to get it together and convince three different appointments today that I am the self-assured answer to their prayers. Hah."

"Well, if it's any comfort to you, you look great. You are the only person on the planet who can get away with those clothes and still look professional." Lil's brows rose as she scanned the black-and-orange outfit.

"I know." Shannon grinned. "It's all in the attitude."

"Add your leopard-print reading glasses and some concealer, and nobody will have a clue you were just bawling."

"Hey, hey, hey. We all know that I am *waaay* too cool to bawl. I just emoted a little bit."

It wasn't in Lilia's nature to snort. But her look said it all.

SOMEHOW, SHANNON MADE IT through the morning and her first two appointments. The first one, Mrs. Drake, was a divorcée who'd recently graduated with honors from law school at age forty-two. She just needed some basic posture lessons—"Shoulders back! Stomach in! Chin up! Project confidence!"—

and help putting together an acceptable corporate wardrobe. She also needed to hear, after twenty years of being put down by her ex, that she was bright, talented and had a great future ahead of her.

Shan loved helping women like Mrs. Drake. She felt such a sense of achievement when, after a few sessions, she sent them out into the world again, reborn in a new skin.

Her second appointment was a teenage girl who looked highly intimidated by her new coach and surroundings. Shannon's heart went out to awkward, homely Janna, and she forgot her own problems. Eyes desperate behind her ugly glasses, Janna confessed that she was in love with a "cool" boy who would never look at her unless Shannon helped her. She was going to pay for her Finesse sessions with her babysitting money, and it seemed all too likely that her mother didn't know she was there.

Shannon hesitated for a moment, debating the ethics. Then she caved in. After all, it wasn't as if she were going to outfit the girl with a thong and spike heels. But take her babysitting money? Shannon couldn't.

"Hold on just a sec, sweetie," she told her. "I've just got to run get some paperwork." She smiled reassuringly and slipped out of her office, closing the door behind her. Moments later, she stood in Jane's office.

"I can't charge this one," she said. "It would be criminal. She's all of fifteen. Isn't there something she can do around the office?"

Jane tapped her pen on her nose.

"Stop that! I thought we broke you of that habit when you drew all over your face."

"Dominic thinks I'm sexy with a Bic mustache. Can the girl type?"

"I don't know."

"Hmm." Jane sat for a moment, thinking, and then brightened. "Mailings! She can help do the direct mail stuff. How about that?"

"Perfect." Shannon spun on her heel, grabbed a generic information form off Jane's credenza and returned to her own office.

"Here we go," she said, handing the sheet of paper to Janna, who peered at it from under her stringy bangs. "If you'll just fill this out, we can get started. The good news is that we've just begun a student discount program. Oh, and by the way, we're looking for someone to help out here a few hours a week. Would you be interested? I know you're not technically employment age, but we could just reduce your bill by the hours you work."

Janna looked as if she might kiss Shannon. Mentally Shan pieced through her closet for a few things that would fit the girl. Babysitting money wouldn't go too far in terms of haircuts, clothes and makeup.

When Janna left, it was noon, which vaguely surprised Shannon. She wasn't hungry. She felt restless, her identity crisis rushing back into her consciousness. Who had actually given birth to her? Where was she now? What did she look like? What nationality was she? What were the circumstances under which she'd had a child—and given her away?

The questions flooded her mind and made her feel unbalanced. She had to get out of here for a while—especially before she faced Hal Underwood, a brain who had single-handedly built his own software company, so successfully that he was now taking it public.

That was impressive. A lot more impressive than failing as an actress; trying to make a living as just one more pretty face in an ocean of them. It also beat out a career grooming people like a monkey.

The unknown Hal Underwood was already giving her an inferiority complex; taking her back to high school where she'd been treated as the stereotypical dumb blonde.

Shannon swept her keys off the corner of her desk and grabbed her lime-green suede hobo bag. "Gotta run some errands!" she called to Lilia and Jane. "Back by one."

She made her way outside, into the gray, chilly Connecticut spring. *Hey, God. Don't you know it's April? Could you improve the weather just a bit?*

Shannon got into her white BMW roadster and put the top down in defiance of the weather. The car, a gift from her *parents,* now seemed all wrong for her. Suddenly she hated it, hated the tan leather seats, hated the logo in the center of the steering wheel, hated the way she must look in the thing: like an expensive, privileged blonde with not a care in the world. What if her real mother was a waitress? A teacher? A postal worker? What if a car like this represented a year's salary to her? The beemer seemed shameful in light of these questions.

She squealed out of the parking lot, the cold April wind in her hair, and headed for Highway 84.

Within moments the sky decided to dump on her, and it seemed fitting. Instead of putting the top up, Shannon let the rain soak her in a cold shower of reality. She pushed the leopard-print reading glasses to the top of her head and drove under the raindrops like a madwoman, not caring what she looked like to others.

Though the rain pelted her face and hair, trickled down the neck of her jacket and damn near froze her in combination with the wind, at least she felt alive. Not numb, as she'd been all afternoon yesterday and all night.

How ironic that I'm an image consultant. Because that's all I am: an image. Everything about my life has been a lie.

4

HAL GRITTED his teeth, still obsessing about the information leak in his company. He'd satisfied himself that it wasn't via an outside hacker, but only after hours upon hours of searching through the logs.

He turned into the Finesse parking lot five minutes early for his one o'clock appointment with Shannon Shane. He did not look forward to it, but he was never, ever late. All of this image b.s. was just another way to waste his time. He had more important things to do, damn it!

He glanced quickly into his rearview mirror to reassure himself once again that he didn't look like Saddam. *Okay, so the beard is bad. The hair is shaggy. But, hey! I have blue eyes. A nice smile, if anyone could see it under the mustache. No signs of mania.*

He got out of his Explorer and walked, in the rain, to the entrance of this place called Finesse. *Pretentious. Fussy. Annoying.* This Shannon person, despite her sense of humor on the phone, would probably be one of those ladies who glided everywhere on high heels, had sprayed-into-place helmet hair and gazed at everyone with a fixed, vacuous smile.

Hal entered the place and said "Hello" to a woman in a beige silk suit. She blinked at him and took an unconscious step backward before returning the greeting. Maybe he *did* look like a terrorist on the run.

"Are you Shannon Shane?" he asked.

"No, I'm sorry, but she's not back from lunch yet. I'm Lilia London, one of Shannon's partners. Won't you have a seat?" She gestured toward a fussy little sofa.

Hal nodded at her and sat down on the awful thing, immediately feeling smothered by the pink cabbage roses on it. It was made for females. Females much smaller than him and with shorter legs.

"Would you like a cup of coffee?" Ms. London asked him.

He shook his head, stared out the window at the parking lot, and began systematically picking at the cuticle on his left thumb.

"You're welcome," he heard her singsong pleasantly under her breath.

He wasn't meant to hear it. He craned his neck after her. "Uh. Uh! Thank you. Too much caffeine today. A gallon for breakfast."

She peered around her office door at him and gave him a very nice smile. "You're welcome."

Hal reverted to a nod again and returned his gaze to the window. *April, huh. Cursed Connecticut. Where is spring?* The rain poured down, relentless.

Hal closed his eyes against the bleak weather and

cracked his neck for tension relief. He flexed his shoulder blades and then opened his eyes to a most peculiar vision.

A white BMW roadster—with the top down!— pulled into Finesse's parking lot next to his Explorer. The driver, a blonde with her wild, curly hair half plastered to her head, seemed in no hurry to get out of the car. She sat there, fingers drumming on the wheel, as if she were enjoying the end of a song on the radio. As if sunshine and blue skies stretched as far as the eye could see, and not gray, chilly pellets of rain.

Nuts. She is completely wacko. The blonde pulled her keys from the ignition, opened the door and slid out two black-leather-covered legs that went up to her armpits. She stood, pushed the door shut, bent over and shook her head like a dog. She walked toward Finesse, her bright orange leather jacket gaping open, *leaving her convertible's top down.*

Forget nuts. That's criminal! But Hal was riveted by her.

The woman stopped just outside the door, under the small green awning. She pulled a pencil out of the breast pocket of her jacket and leaned over again, shaking water from her hair onto the sidewalk. She twisted the wet, curly mass and wrung it out. More water puddled around her black spike-heeled boots.

As he watched, fascinated, she secured her hair into a knot with the pencil pushed through it and righted herself. Then she opened the door.

Hal got up from among the cabbage roses and addressed her as soon as she walked in. "You left your top down."

"Hi," she said, with an engaging smile. "You must be Saddam."

"S—? Uh, yeah." Hal pointed outside. "Your car!"

"I know, thanks. It will be fine."

No, it won't, you crazy woman. But you sure are…

"Thanks for pointing it out, though." Her white tailored blouse was soaked and transparent. Hal tried his best not to look, but her nipples showed right through. His cheeks warmed. So did other parts of him.

"Your seats," he said. "The car will be flooded."

She shrugged. "So be it."

She was Amazon perfection. Green cat eyes, delicate little nose, lips to make a man sob. Her breasts were full and taut; held in place by an unusual, unpadded bra. He could see little multicolored happy faces with tongues on it. *Tongues.* "Would you like me to go out and put the top up for you?" *Do her panties match?*

"No, thank you. Really, it's fine." She looked him over from head to toes—not rudely, just appraisingly. "I'm Shannon, by the way."

He put a hand up to his face self-consciously. He couldn't believe he was thinking about this woman's panties within thirty seconds of meeting her! Peg was right. He'd been dating his computer for too long. But Shannon Shane was stunning. No other word for it.

Hal felt as though he was back in high school, gazing at the head cheerleader without a prayer. Cruel, cool blondes had surrounded him in his dreams then, laughing and pointing at him while he stood naked and tried to hide his sexual longing behind his hands.

He was once again the skinny dork behind the heavy glasses. The victim of a cruel prom prank that he never wanted to think about again. Samantha Stanton. Shannon Shane reminded him of Sam Stanton, possessor of a sadistic streak a mile wide—and too cool for school.

He braced himself, locked his knees unconsciously. Stuck out his hand without a trace of warmth. "Hal Underwood, aka Saddam," he said. "Reporting for cleanup. Shall we begin interrogations?"

She cocked her head at him in silent evaluation. "Sure thing. Right after I find a towel." She showed him into her office and gestured to the visitor's chair opposite her desk. "Be right back."

Hal tried not to notice her black-leather-clad rear end as it swung out the door but it screamed provocation and juicy, bad-girl, no-holds-barred sex. So much for his preconception of her. What kind of woman dressed like that for the office? Now hard as a rock, he needed to distract himself and...deflate.

He looked around her office. It shouted L.A. or Miami, not Farmington, Connecticut. For one thing, the walls were tangerine, and upon them hung framed black-and-white portraits of famous actors and actresses. A few framed and signed record albums were scattered artistically among them, adding color. In one corner stood a…what the hell *was* it? He didn't know, exactly, but he liked it. A cross between a scooter, a bicycle and a lateral pull-down machine, the thing was painted in primary colors and splashed with secondaries like purple, turquoise, orange and lime-green. Hal tried, but failed, to discern any use for the creation. Maybe it was some mod, wild sex toy? There went his mind again, straight into the gutter.

His gaze moved to Shannon Shane's desk, which consisted of a huge sheet of thick, beveled glass resting on four tall, hand-blown Murano vases. How she had found four different vases of exactly the same height, he didn't know. He questioned the stability of the desk—not to mention the stability of its owner.

Behind the desk a Dr. Seuss calendar hung on the wall. How apropos. Hal had often wondered what the good doctor smoked, but the man never failed to make him smile. His gaze returned to the leather chair, and his mind to the gutter. He saw himself in the chair, with Shannon Shane astride him wearing nothing but that orange leather jacket.

Shannon chose this moment to return to the room with her jacket zipped over the wet shirt and happy-face bra. Thank God. He was hard enough without having to ogle the woman's breasts. Not that he'd mind, exactly.

"So, Saddam," she said. "I apologize for being late and wet."

Wet. He almost groaned aloud. What was wrong with him?

"I got caught on the highway with the top down."

"That's okay," Hal said.

He refrained from mentioning that there was a little button in her car that would have taken care of the problem. He wished he had a little button to take care of his.

Hal looked at the bizarre object in the corner again and pointed to it. "What *is* that?"

Shannon laughed. "That is a work of art by up-and-coming sculptor Gilbey O'Toole."

"Ah."

"Do you like it?"

Hal nodded slowly. "Yes, I do. I was just a little mystified."

"It reminds me of something Dr. Seuss would build. I love it. And Gilbey is the brother of a good friend of mine."

Hal sat silent, unable to think of much to say, besides "Take me now!" which even *he* knew was socially unacceptable.

"He had a big show in Boston," she continued.

Hal looked at her.

"And he sold every piece. He's got another coming up in New York."

She gazed at Hal expectantly.

"Uh. Great," he said. God, those long, leather-clad legs...

They sat for another long moment. Shannon spun

in her chair and pulled a legal pad from a drawer in her credenza. She made a note on it.

Hal read it upside down. *Small talk,* she'd written. Wonderful. She was noting down his failings while he drooled over her.

"I don't like small talk," he said. "It's a waste of time."

Shannon caught her top lip between her teeth. "Okay. Then why don't we get straight to the point of why you're here. Various people have ganged up on you—your mom, your sister… Why do you think they're doing that? And why now?"

"I'm in the process of taking my company public. The underwriters are in full swing right now. I can't really talk about it. But my legal advisor is on this tangent about how I'm the face of the company, and the future rests upon me…blah, blah, blah."

"And what about Mom and Sis?"

"Yeah." Hal looked down. "My mother wants me to produce hairless microhumans." *All I want to do is practice. With you.*

"Excuse me?"

"Babies. Mom wants grandchildren. My sister just wants me to have a social life." *God, I sound like such a dweeb.* Again, he was back in high school, being picked on by the Beautiful People. Except this was worse. He was now (figuratively) on his knees before a Beautiful Person, offering to pay her to de-dork him. *Painful. This is just painful.* Inside, Hal cringed. Outside, he just blinked at her.

"What do *you* want, Hal?"

Amazing. She didn't seem to be laughing at him at all. Probably because there was a fat check involved. "What do I want? Well, primarily I want my company to succeed. And I want them all off my back."

And I want to find out who's leaking information to my competition. No way did Greer Conover develop a prototype, on his own, that's just like ours. Conover had always been a sneak and a slime, and he'd frequently cheated off Hal's tests in college.

"Okay," said Shannon. "Then we're looking at a multistage process. First we need to work on some surface stuff like a haircut, a shave and some new clothes."

"I was afraid of that."

"Painless, I promise."

"Uh-huh." She had a beautiful smile and because of it, he didn't trust a word she said. The smile was a tool.

"And by the way, underneath all that hair, I think you're much better-looking than Saddam."

Lay it on thick, baby, so I'll write you a check. He flashed her a sardonic glance. "That's not saying much."

She laughed. "Okay, during stage two we'll work on things like small talk and posture and media training. And during stage three, I'll teach you how to become irresistible to women."

"Irresistible, huh?"

"Absolutely." Her voice was firm. Again, no trace of amusement. A damn good actress, was Shannon Shane.

"All this in the next thirty days?"

She nodded.

Hal sighed. "When do we start and how much is all this going to cost me?"

She looked at her watch, a platinum number that had probably cost some sucker boyfriend more than Hal paid Tina, his receptionist, in a year. "We start now. I made a tentative appointment with a stylist for you. He's a good friend of mine, so he held a slot open."

Stylist? The very word sounded ominous to Hal. Expensive and suspicious. "I go to a barber close to my office."

"Not anymore, you don't." She gave him a sunny smile. Then she named a ballpark sum for her services that scandalized him.

Hal's jaw dropped open. "Do you know how many computers I could buy for that money?"

She met his gaze squarely. "You don't need any more computers. Do you?"

Hey, a guy could *always* use more computers. He would admit nothing.

"And you *do* need a new image, right?"

A matter of opinion.

"So you're going to need a lot of coaching, good suits for media interviews, new glasses, new shoes—"

"No penny loafers." Hal laid down the law.

"What?"

"Don't even try."

"*Penny loafers?* No, of course not. Nobody but a

dyed-in-the-wool, New England preppy would wear those things. We're going for a much more hip, intellectual but sexy image."

Hal almost laughed at the idea that he could ever be hip or sexy. He looked again at Shannon Shane's Dr. Seuss wall calendar. She was a kook. A gorgeous kook. But she wasn't going to make him wear penny loafers.

"All right," he sighed. And against his inclination and better judgment, he placed himself in Shannon's too-beautiful hands.

5

SHANNON FELT LIKE A FRAUD, a farce and a failure. And all the orange leather jackets in the world couldn't change the facts: she, a failed actress, was nothing compared to someone like Hal Underwood, a guy so brilliant that he'd not only founded his own software company but was about to take it public.

Sure, she could help him with his public image. If only he could help her with her private one. People never got past her surface. For as long as she could remember, she'd been a victim of stares from both sexes. The stares of men were at best admiring and at worst downright lustful. The stares of women were usually hostile, envious or despairing.

She'd gotten used to being looked at—after all, there was nothing she could do about it—but she'd never get used to the strange emotions her appearance produced in other people. And she'd never grow accustomed to the feeling that nobody ever heard a word she said—they simply watched her lips move. Worse—she now didn't even know who she was, and therefore what she had to say.

Since her car was flooded, they took Hal's to see Enrique, her stylist.

His salon was a sumptuous ode to blue velvet. The curved reception desk was upholstered in a deep navy, as was the long sofa. Various chairs and pillows ranged in hue from royal to turquoise to periwinkle. Even the cornice boards were turquoise velvet.

A tall vase of peacock feathers stood in one corner, and on the one wall that wasn't dominated by gilt mirrors hung every employee's state cosmetology license framed in monstrously ornate gold.

Shannon had gotten used to Enrique's royal environment. Hal stood like a deer in the headlights and gazed in stupefaction at the Early Bordello decor while Enrique danced out to greet them.

"'Allo, beeeyoootiful," he said to Shannon.

"Hi, Enrique." She kissed him on the cheek. "How are you?"

"Bueno." A small, vivacious man who barely reached to Shannon's shoulders, he assessed Hal with great interest. He stroked his chin. He tapped his foot. He walked around him in a circle and peered at him.

"I theenk we have good things under all thees hair, my friend."

Hal hunched his shoulders and sent a desperate look to Shannon. It clearly said, "Get me outta here!"

She smiled.

"Come!" ordered Enrique. "You seet here, in my chair." He looped his arm through Hal's, to the poor guy's discomfort, and dragged him off to his lair. Shannon repressed a giggle and followed.

"First, we shave, yes?" Enrique tugged on Hal's beard.

"Ow!"

"Is no a good look for you. Off!" The stylist brandished an old-fashioned razor.

"Uh," said Hal, fingering his neck. "Why not let me do that?"

"No, no. Is for you to relax." The little man pushed him into a salon chair and immediately flipped it back to a lounging position. Within moments, he had his victim's face smothered in shaving cream and was scraping away. Hal looked about as relaxed as a lobster being held over a pot of boiling water.

As Enrique scraped, he hummed tunelessly, achieving a virtually indescribable sound. Shannon concentrated on describing it anyway, so she wouldn't laugh at the panicked expression in Hal's eyes, and came up with Ricky Martin meets whale calls.

"Enrique may slaughter a tune, but he won't slit your throat," she reassured Hal.

The man who emerged from under all the white lather fifteen minutes later had high cheekbones, a strong jaw and a full lower lip. Paired with those blue eyes, even behind his cheesy glasses, the combination was striking. Shannon couldn't help staring. Hal didn't look at all like Saddam. He looked…good. Really good.

Enrique snatched off Hal's glasses and then took

the poor man's face between his hands and turned it this way and that. He smoothed back the overgrown, shaggy hair, pursed his lips and cocked his head. *"Sí!"* he announced, to no one in particular.

"Sí?" Shannon asked. "Do you think a Caesar cut, or a little longer on top?"

"Caesar, yes, he has the bones for it."

"He does?" asked Hal. "I mean, I do?"

"Yes, yes!"

"I'm not so sure about th…" Hal trailed off as great whacks of hair began to fall at Enrique's feet. "Wait—"

"Be calm. You are in the presence of genius," Shannon assured him.

"Yes, me! Genius! That ees so." Enrique practically danced as he worked, fingers flying.

Hal closed his eyes and seemed to be praying. More hair flew as the stylist's scissors flashed.

When the menacing chops ceased, Hal opened his eyes again and fished for his glasses, settling them onto his nose. He had become a different person, and judging from his expression, he couldn't quite believe it.

For her part, she was floored. Hal was hot!

Enrique allowed the spectacles back on with a frown. He still snipped and fussed and compared lengths of hair in his fingers, but he seemed pleased. Hal stared at the stranger in the mirror.

Shannon stared, too.

"Bueno!" Enrique exclaimed. "Behold Caesar!"

Shannon doubted that the great Julius had ever worn a polyester-blend plaid shirt or hideous glasses, but she didn't contradict the stylist, who was clearly proud of himself.

Hal, still squinting into the mirror in disbelief, muttered something about the Ides of March.

Enrique made a dive for his glasses again, but Hal blocked him.

"Off!" the little man insisted. "These must go goodbye-bye. They *ruin* my brilliance. You get the contacts, eh?"

Shannon nodded. "Next stop, Fashionocular."

Hal began to protest but was soon felled into silence by the magnitude of Enrique's bill. Shannon hid another smile as he goggled at the charge.

"You're kidding me," he croaked. "This is *robbery!*"

Enrique drew himself to his full height of five foot nothing and puffed up like a blowfish. *"Perdón?"* His tone was ominous. "Rrrrobbery?"

Hal stood his ground. *"Larceny."*

Enrique tilted his head to the side and narrowed his black eyes. "Eh? I no familiar weeth thees word. But is obvious rrrrude."

Hal looked again at the charge slip and didn't deny it.

The stylist whirled on one foot, his chest heaving, and glared at Shannon. "He takes back thees insults, or—" he stooped to the salon floor and gathered up two fistfuls of hair "—I glue back thees hairs to his face!"

Shannon laid a hand on the enraged man's arm,

but he shook it off, casting the hair clippings into Hal's open mouth.

While he blinked, shocked, and spat them out, she said quickly, "Enrique! He didn't mean it. Robbery—it's just a turn of phrase. Cute. You know, ha-ha! Hal here was making a joke. Weren't you, Hal?"

"Uh, no," he said, blue eyes stormy. He pulled more hairs off his tongue and lower lip. "No, I was *not* making a joke."

Enrique hissed like an angry Latin goose.

"Hal!"

"What?"

"You're not making this situation any better." She dug into her hobo bag for her wallet, pushing him out the door of the salon. "Wait for me outside while I pay him and try to salvage my relationship with the only top stylist this side of New York!"

As HAL WATCHED through the glass door, arms crossed and foot tapping, a silent Shakespearean tragedy unfolded inside. Shannon's lips moved earnestly while Enrique's back remained steadfastly turned to her. She kept speaking until his shoulder eased a quarter turn in her direction, and he finally nodded.

She waved an obscene wad of cash at him, but he shook his head and made her talk to The Hand. Patiently she entreated his palm until he apparently got tired of extending it, since he rubbed at his bicep.

Hal snorted.

Shannon next said something to Enrique that actually made him smile, though his lips turned downward again and his nose went up as soon as he beheld Hal through the glass. She added a phrase.

Enrique gestured at him in obvious disgust and then nodded. The stylist finally snatched the cash, kissed Shannon's cheek and strutted off, this time like an insulted rooster.

She opened the door, emerged, and then sagged against it, eyeing Hal with severity.

Uh-oh. He didn't care much about Enrique, but he'd gone and pissed off the Goddess. Would she zap him with a moon ray, or something? Turn him into a fire hydrant frequented by neighborhood dogs? He squinted balefully at her jacket, at the way her glossy blond hair slid over it and beckoned his gaze to exactly breast level. He looked away from the forbidden zone.

"Tact, Hal. I know it's a four-letter word, but you need to get some. You put me in a really bad position with Enrique, back there."

Hal could practically feel his jaw jutting out in stubborn righteousness.

"He's very proud of his work, and he's cut the hair of a lot of bigwigs, no pun intended. You can't tell him that what he charges is robbery!"

"But—"

"It would be like one of your clients saying *you* overcharge. That your software is garbage."

Hal chuckled. "Never. That just wouldn't happen."

"Uh-huh. Well, I don't think Enrique's ever had it happen, either. Have you *looked at yourself,* by the way? He's worth every penny!"

"So he cut a few inches off my mop. And what is this Caesar crap all about? Please tell me you're not hauling me off to be fitted for a toga and ankle-wrap sandals next?"

Shannon's lips twitched. "No. But believe me, Enrique did a lot more than chop a few inches. He's truly an artist."

Snort. "I still don't see why he's worth six times what my regular barber charges." Hal raked his fingers through the new Caesar cut, frowning. "I should charge *him*—he kept a lot of my hair! He probably runs a good racket selling the stuff for toupees out his back door."

Shannon closed her lovely green eyes briefly. "Enrique does *not* sell clippings for hairpieces, I can assure you…."

Though he saw annoyance sparkling and radiating from her irises, he also discerned amusement. Was this Amazon sex goddess *laughing* at him again, on top of everything? The situation just sucked, plain and simple. He was going to wring Peggy's neck for getting him into this.

They reached his Explorer and Hal walked around to the passenger side to unlock and open Shannon's door for her. He supposed it was one of those things a goddess expected. She climbed into the truck one long leg at a time, and he tried not to notice the delicate musculature revealed under the leather pants. Tried to ignore the more interesting creases and crevices where the lucky pants rode her hips and thighs. He failed.

He gave himself a stern internal lecture.

This woman is nothing but a torment sent by my sister and a scourge upon my bank account. I am not interested in her pants or anything inside them.

Like most lectures, it went ignored. Not only was he lying to himself, but he was hard again.

6

HAL SWUNG INTO the driver's seat, started the ignition and checked the rearview mirror before backing out of his parking spot. What the hell? Who the hell? Oh. It was him. His new appearance was going to take some getting used to.

"Okay," said Shannon, his tormentor and scourge. "You want to head toward Avon, Hal."

He had a strong suspicion that he didn't want to do that at all. "Why?"

"We're going to update your eyewear now."

"I just got these glasses a year and a half ago. I don't need new ones."

She blinked rapidly. "The frames are new, too, or just the lenses?"

"The lenses."

"That's what I thought. Those frames date back to about 1989, don't they?"

"Uh…"

"Never mind." Shannon reached over and cupped his jaw, tilted his chin toward her.

Hey, I'm trying to drive, here, woman! But he

didn't say it. The touch of her fingertips awakened exhilaration in him, plucked at some hidden longing that he didn't want to acknowledge. A sweet lemon scent tickled his nostrils—her hand lotion?

"We need something smaller, lighter, with a more rectangular shape," she said, after moistening her lips.

Was it his imagination or had her eyes gone smoky for an instant? *No, what we need is to get naked right here on Route 4.* Hal jerked his gaze back to the road.

"And I'd like you to try a set of contact lenses."

"No. They irritate my eyes and drive me crazy."

"When was the last time you tried them?"

"College."

"They've made some improvements since then. Some of the new extended-wear lenses are so thin and flexible that you can't even feel them."

Hal sighed and kept driving. He had a feeling it was going to be a long day, and every moment spent with Shannon Shane was time he wasn't tracking the source of his information leak. If he didn't find it before the IPO... Such a possibility didn't bear thinking about.

He put a hand up to tug on the whiskers normally abundant on his chin. Damn it! Nothing but skin. How far would this transformation go? The back of his neck was cold, too, and his head felt lighter. Hal wondered if this was how a sheep felt after its wool got harvested.

He looked over at the source of his torment, but Shannon now seemed lost in a world of her own. The fingers of her left hand drummed restlessly on the leather seat between them, every now and then gripping the edge and then losing purchase, falling back to the cushion. The drumming began again seconds later. Her smooth olive skin stretched taut across the fine bones, seeming to barely contain her energy.

She seemed disturbed, deep in thought, trying to come to terms with something.

What went on in the brain of a goddess? Hal found himself vaguely surprised that he wondered. For surely goddesses didn't ponder much—they just accepted the worship of others as their due and basked in the glory.

Shannon was obviously not in the least dim, but he doubted that she was contemplating the philosophy of Nietzsche or Kant.

She roused herself out of her reverie long enough to give him adequate directions, and soon they were turning into the strip mall that housed Fashionocular, scene of his next trial by fire.

The vague sense of doom hanging over Hal morphed immediately into dismay as he followed Shannon through the door. Hundreds—thousands?—of blank spectacles met his gaze, rows upon rows of them, running from floor to forehead level. He'd never seen so many at once. He'd always bought his glasses at one of the lower-end department stores, and had never chosen from more than perhaps fifty styles.

He looked around. Horn-rims, wire-rims, plastic-rims of every possible width. Round lenses, cat's-eye lenses, elliptical lenses, rectangular ones. And you could see the world in any hue: blue, green, yellow, tan, pink or even purple. The frames all stared at him, mocked him, disembodied though they were.

"I can't possibly try all these on," he said to Shannon. "I'd need hours...even days."

"Of course not," she said. "You're going to work with Marta, trying on different contacts, while I select between five and ten pairs. Okay?"

"But I don't want to stick little bits of plastic onto my eyeballs. I told you that...."

She nodded until he wound down a bit, feeling that she'd actually listened to him this time. Then she stuck a finger in his back and propelled him toward a plump, pleasant-looking woman.

"Marta? This is Hal Underwood. He's a little squeamish about contact lenses, but I think he's only tried the hard ones, years ago. I'm putting him into your care."

"Hi, Mr. Underwood. We've got all kinds of soft lenses now that you can't even feel, I promise. And look how handsome you are! Why would you hide that face behind glasses?" She smiled flirtatiously at him.

Handsome? The woman was hallucinating. Or more likely, Shannon paid her to butter up the clients she brought in.

Muttering to himself, and wondering when he could get back to his office and pursue more worthwhile things than his appearance, Hal sat in a squat rolling chair in front of a counter that held a circular, magnified mirror. Marta asked what his vision was—20/600 in the left eye and 20/740 in the right—and then brought out several little boxes and sanitized her hands.

Then she reached with her forefinger and thumb into the tiny well of a contact case, and came up with something that looked exactly like a round piece of plastic wrap.

Hal stared at it.

"It's painless, really," Marta promised. "You put it on your index finger, like this, and add a drop of solution. Then guide it into your eye and blink."

He grimaced. "And then how in the hell do I get it *out?*"

She dimpled and demonstrated. "You'll grasp it just like this and pluck, presto."

Yeah. Pluck, presto. Hal had a feeling he would die with the little pieces of Glad wrap still on his corneas. He hoped they were sticky so they'd hold the coins over his eyes when he got buried.

But aside from some blinking to get rid of excess solution, he had to admit the lenses were comfortable—and he even saw more clearly. His old glasses had obviously not been strong enough. He felt absolutely nothing in his eyes, and accepted Marta's recommendation of two-week extended-wear contacts.

Hal peered at himself in the mirror, still shocked at his changed appearance. He'd noticed before that the little Latin bandit Enrique had left his hair in uneven but somehow choreographed chops and wisps. He touched it, mildly revolted by the waxy, sticky goop the stylist had worked in.

But, well...look at that. He had Brad Pitt's hair, if not his box office draw. Especially without the glasses, and with his new improved vision, he didn't look half bad. Huh. Now if he could only find the source of the info leak, he'd be One Hundred Percent Man.

SHANNON SHORED UP her initial assault with a half dozen choices in designer eyewear. She cornered a reluctant Hal and slipped them on and off his face. Really, it was quite amazing how different he looked in each pair. More and more sophisticated. More and more confident—even authoritarian.

She debated between the last two pairs: one with a heavier, dark rectangular frame and the other with a lighter, more streamlined rimless frame.

"Hal, do you have any preference?"

"Nope," he said. "I just want to be able to see."

She decided in favor of the heavier frame. His strong angular jaw balanced out the glasses well, and they gave him an aura of power. Pair them with that hair, a little stubble, a black cashmere V-neck and... yum. You could find yourself wanting to skinny-dip in those Bahama-blue eyes of his.

He cleared his throat and looked away.

Shannon realized with a start that she'd been staring at him for about five minutes straight, and blinked. Come to think of it, he'd been staring at her, too.

And he'd been looking *inside,* trying to figure her out, not slobbering over her body and thinking of dragging her off to a cave by the hair. After years of experience, she could tell the difference.

She pushed the thought away and told Marta which frames they'd purchase. And then she braced herself, because with the nonglare coating, the shatterproof glass, the cool sunshade attachment and the costly designer frames, Hal was going to—

"Whaaaat?! *How* much did you say?"

—have an aneurism and a heart attack all at once.

"YES, BUT WHAT YOU'RE NOT understanding, Hal," she told him in the privacy of the Explorer, "is that Marta can't help the prices! She doesn't make them up, she just works there. And you make her feel really bad when you squawk over the total."

"Well, it makes me feel really bad, too! Who pays over six hundred dollars for a pair of glasses? I don't see any diamond studs in them...."

"Hal, listen to me. You're paying for a whole image, here. You're essentially going to be advertising for your company, and you want to project an image of intelligence, decisiveness, sophistication. You want people to have confidence in your work, so—"

"So I'll show them the damned product. Why does it matter what I look like? Is our society really that shallow? I should be able to do my own at-home, bowl-over-the-head haircut and wear glasses frames fashioned from a coat hanger! None of this has anything to do with how good I am or how effective my software will be in streamlining business processes. This is bullsh—"

Shannon threw up her hands. "Should, should, should," she said, exasperated. "In an idealistic world, Hal, all of that would be true. But that's not the kind of planet we live on." She blew out a breath, shook her head and twisted her hair into a knot. She dug into her bag for a pencil and secured the curly mass on her head.

"Look. Why don't you take me back to Finesse, okay? It's obvious that you're completely hostile to this whole process, and quite frankly you're hurting *my* feelings at this point. I'm just trying to do my job, not bilk you of your life savings."

They rode in silence for a few minutes. Out of the corner of her eye, she watched a muscle jump in Hal's jaw. She turned away and looked out the window instead, at the road rushing under them like gray flannel, the grass an emerald blur, telephone poles whizzing by like matchsticks. The neat Cape Cods became pale flashes, their unique weathered charms lost in a fog of succession.

Did her birth mother live in one of those? Or in some stucco place in Florida? A limestone house in Texas? A ski chalet in Utah or Colorado?

Hal's voice reached her on her imaginary journeys. "I'm sorry," he said. "I didn't mean to make you feel bad." He reached out and put his hand on her arm.

A frisson of strange awareness shot through her.

She turned to him, surprised. It was rare, in her experience, for a man to apologize. His gaze bored into hers, and again she had the feeling he saw far more than she was used to.

He had a small mole in the middle of his right cheek—on a woman it would have been called a beauty mark—and she found herself wanting to touch it. She did no such thing.

"I know," she said. "Thanks."

He nodded and she let the noises of the car comfort and steady her. The sound of the wind rushing past, the rumble of the engine, the muffled tap of brakes as they slowed for a turning vehicle ahead.

"Did you grow up around here, Shannon?"

The question caught her by surprise. "Close." She hesitated, anticipating his reaction. "Greenwich." A lot of people assumed she was a snob when she told them she grew up there.

"Interesting. You don't seem like the Greenwich type."

"I'm not." She left it at that.

"How did you get into this line of work?"

"Oh. Well, a friend suggested it, actually. My friend Jane, who's a co-owner of Finesse. We were all in dead-end jobs—at least they were—I was just a miserably failing actress, out in L.A. with a hundred thousand of them." She laughed self-consciously.

"That takes guts," Hal said.

"No. It takes naiveté and delusion." She chuckled again, but even to her own ears it sounded forced.

"You can call it what you want to, but I call it courage. To put your dream on the line like that, to move away from everything familiar…"

I could kiss him. The thought didn't shock her as much as it should have. *I could kiss him for saying that to me right now. It's like he knows how badly I need to hear it.*

They had turned into the parking lot of Finesse, and Hal idled the truck near her sodden car, the only other one in the small lot.

"Thank you," she said to him. Then she leaned over and acted on her thought.

7

SHANNON'S URGE TO KISS Hal had appeared impulsively out of nowhere, and as far as kisses went it was supposed to be friendly, quick and not too personal.

But when her lips touched his cheek he turned in surprise, making full mouth contact with her. An electric current shot through her, lighting her like a Christmas tree, even though he sat frozen for a long moment.

But then his lips grew hungry and surprisingly, he took over the kiss. His mouth hard on her mouth, he slipped his tongue between her lips and pulled her across the front seat of the SUV, one hand on the small of her back and the other on her bottom.

The electricity hit her again, shaking her as he pulled her into his lap and against an erection that would have done a bull proud.

Warning bells went off in her head, and Shannon started to pull away so that she didn't give Hal the completely wrong idea. But instead of grinding himself against her or even trying to force her head down toward his zipper, he simply took her face into his hands and kissed each of her eyelids, then her mouth again.

He was so gentle as he coaxed another response out of her, slid his seeking tongue into her mouth again and made love to it.

He made no move to touch her breasts, no lunges toward other private parts of her anatomy. And the irony of the situation was that, after dodging countless numbers of gropers over the years, Shannon wished that Hal *would* touch her breasts.

At the moment, they were tightly zipped into her orange jacket and squashed against his chest. They felt heavy and the peaks throbbed with longing, aching as much as the core of her.

"Unzip my jacket," she said huskily. "Touch me."

He raised his head and looked into her eyes. "Are you sure that's what you want?"

"Yes."

Still he hesitated, searching her eyes for something, she didn't know what. "Why?" he finally asked.

"Because you're here," she said. "And hot." She ran a hand along his erection. "And hard." She mentioned nothing about the endless, hopeless circles of questions rolling through her head. Nothing about needing distraction, comfort, a reminder that she, the child who'd been given away, was desired.

All she wanted right now was some steamy, mindless sex. She wanted the questions sucked from her erogenous zones, kneaded from her flesh, pounded out of her by an insistent physical rhythm building to a frenzied peak.

Hal's hand went to her zipper, his breathing labored, his eyes slightly glazed. Still he hesitated. "Why me?" he asked, his voice thick.

Shannon straddled him and rubbed herself shamelessly against his hard-on. "Hal, honey. Just be a good boy and don't question your luck. It's a gift, okay? Now shut up and take it."

HE SHUT UP AND TOOK HER. Inside her office, where her partners were nowhere to be seen on a Saturday evening. She unlocked the door, his hands hot on her behind, even through the leather pants. He allowed her to draw the blinds, and then to her delighted shock, he took over. Hal backed her against the unused reception desk, picked her up and set her on it. Then he pulled down the zipper on her jacket with his teeth and ripped open her still-damp white blouse to bare her breasts in the happy-face bra. He undid the front clasp and murmured his appreciation. Then he pushed her back against the surface of the desk and took one in his mouth.

She moaned and moved restlessly at the hot, wet suction around her nipple, his tongue flicking against it and his hand massaging the other one. Her own hands moved to his shoulders and down his arms, surprisingly muscular for a computer geek.

He caught her wrists and held them prisoner while he suckled her other breast and then leisurely unsnapped and unzipped her leather pants.

"My boots," she protested.

"The boots are the only things that stay on, gorgeous." And Hal stripped off everything else she was wearing except for her tiny happy-face thong. The jacket flew to one corner, the blouse to another. Her bra landed midfloor, while Hal seemed to savor sliding her pants down her legs and then, slowly, over the black, spike-heeled boots.

He tossed the pants onto the floor, kneeling in front of her and looking up the length of her calves and thighs with something close to awe.

Maybe it was literally having a man at her feet, looking as if he wanted to devour every inch of her, but as she sat before him in nothing but her boots and a thong, Shannon's nipples hardened and she grew wet under his gaze.

"Now, put your feet on my shoulders and spread your legs for me. Just go easy with those spike heels."

Shannon put one foot on his shoulder and watched as he enjoyed the view. "You take your clothes off, now."

He turned his face toward her thigh and nipped it gently, then licked upward as she grew impossibly wetter. "'Kay," he agreed. He shrugged out of his jacket and peeled his shirt off.

Hal without a shirt was a very pleasant surprise. Though he obviously hadn't seen the sun in months, and his posture was normally terrible, he had the build of a swimmer and no flab on him.

But Hal without his pants...who knew? Who could possibly have predicted the dot-com nerd was hung like *that?* He was thick and muscular and completely at attention, his focus unwavering on her.

Shannon's insides melted at the sight. She put her other foot on Hal's shoulder, obeying orders. He grinned wickedly at her and tugged her forward on the slick surface of the desk. She could feel his breath at the very center of her, through the flimsy fabric of her thong. But he didn't touch.

Touching was reserved for her breasts, and as he rose to take her nipples again into his mouth, her feet rose with him, slipped off his shoulders and eventually down around his waist.

Once he'd reduced her to a whimpering puddle of need just through her nipples, Hal sank onto his knees again and focused on the prize right in front of him. He spread her thighs as wide as he could and dipped his head to the core of her, slipping his tongue under the fabric of her thong.

She convulsed at the contact, gasping, and he gripped her buttocks to steady her and hold her in place. Then he went to work in earnest, slicking his tongue over her and around her lips, between them, over them. He sucked the most sensitive part of her into his mouth and played it expertly.

Hot rushes of sensation pooled there and licked at every erogenous point on her body. She could feel tension building and spiraling in her belly while he toyed with her clitoris and menaced any vestiges of self-control she had left.

"Please," she begged. "I want you inside, Hal, before I lose it…"

The words were hardly out her mouth when he'd ripped off her thong and somehow sheathed himself in a condom. She didn't know how or where it had come from, but frankly she didn't care.

All she cared about was the way it felt when he entered her, filled her, stretched her. She was so wet that he slid in immediately with no awkwardness and began to pump deep within her.

He was a hot, hard, slick piston driving inside and awakening some answering rhythm in her body. She slid her hands up and down his back; allowed them to fall to his buttocks, which were rigid with tension and muscle mass.

She rode him, and he rode her, for minutes more. Then the tension finally culminated and broke into a hot explosion of brilliant color and gratitude.

Shannon collapsed against the desk, loving her new fashion statement: nothing but boots and a naked man.

HAL'S LIBIDO was intensely grateful for Shannon's unexpected *gift*, especially as he still lay on top of her and inside her.

Hal's ego, however, was another matter entirely. *Why?* he'd asked.

Because you're here….

Why me? he'd said to her.

Just be a good boy and don't question your luck.

He couldn't shake the ugly feeling that he'd been

used to scratch the goddess's itch. If he hadn't been around, she might have chosen a gas station attendant, or a bank teller. Anyone with the right equipment for the job: a fairly hefty hard-on.

He shriveled with the realization and rolled off Shannon to find his pants.

She yawned and stretched before sitting up. "You've got a really cute butt, Hal."

"Uh," he said, starting to feel like a piece of meat. *Does that mean she wants to sprinkle my ass with salt and pepper and throw it on the grill?*

"And an impressive knowledge of the female anatomy." She grinned.

"Well, thank you. Glad I could be…of service." He glanced at her and saw that the grin had faded. Her eyes narrowed, too, at his tone.

"What's the matter, Hal? You don't respect me now?" She twisted her long, curly hair into a knot on top of her head.

"I respect you just fine." He wrestled into his shirt and tried not to get turned on by her all over again, while she stood naked except for those dominatrix boots. "I'm just, uh, cowed by your beauty, that's all." His tone was drier than dust.

That comment seemed to upset her. "Let's leave my looks out of this, shall we?" Then she snorted. "Except we can't. That's why you did me, isn't it. Because of what I look like."

"No, Shannon." He said it quietly. "If you remember, I asked you if this was what you wanted, if you were sure. *You* did *me.* And I have to wonder why. Because I was *here,* you said. That's very flattering."

Hal shrugged into his jacket and jammed his feet into his shoes. "Tell you what. Next time you've got an itch that needs scratching, I'll drop you off at the local Wal-Mart and you can pick up the greeter."

She opened and closed her mouth.

He fully expected her to throw something at him. Maybe beat the crap out of him. Knock him down and put one of those spike heels through his eye socket.

The last thing he expected was for the goddess's lip to tremble, her nose to turn bright pink or her face to crumple. The very last thing he had anticipated was for Shannon Shane, Queen of L.A. Cool, to burst into tears.

But she did. She wept as she tried to put her thong back on, realized it was ripped to hell, and shoved it into the pocket of her black leather pants. She dotted those with tears as she slid them up her long legs and over her delectable bottom. She cried on her blouse, which she had to tie together since he'd eviscerated all the buttons. And she snarled through tear-filled eyes as he tried to hold her jacket out for her. "Go away!"

"Shannon—"

"No."

"I'm sorry. I take that last comment back."

"No, you don't."

"I do. I said it in anger, basically. It came straight

from my ego. I—" He cracked his neck. "Shit. I figure, a beautiful girl decides to have her way with me, she must be using me because I'm not much to look at."

"I wasn't using you," she sobbed. "I was using… the sex. To feel better."

"Oh," said Hal. Then he laughed mirthlessly. "That's even better. I could have been a damned dildo."

"What? No! Oh, God…" Shannon couldn't speak for a few moments. When she recovered, she gripped his arm. "That's not what I meant. Hal, first of all I don't sleep with people very often. Second, I only sleep with people I'm very attracted to. And third, I'm feeling very emotionally screwed up right now and…and…I was looking for whatever comfort I could find."

He found a box of tissue on the windowsill and handed it to her. *Christ. So I've gone from dildo to teddy bear. Which is worse?*

Shannon blew her nose and Hal stared at her, wondering why he found her even more appealing with the swollen red nose and puffy pink eyes. He took a couple of steps closer to her and zipped up her jacket, since she was utterly indecent in the buttonless blouse. Then he tipped up her chin. "Why are you feeling screwed up?"

She sniffled and shrugged.

"'Cause it seems to me that you should be feeling scrumptiously screwed, but not screwed *up*."

He received a glimmer of a smile for this attempt

at lightness. He pressed on. "I think I've figured out that you don't mean to be breathtakingly rude. So you didn't mean to call me a dildo or a pacifier, right?

"I figure this takes great perception and tolerance on my part. Or stupidity. Anyway, I'm still talking to you. So why don't you tell me what's wrong?"

Can anything be wrong in the life of a woman who looks like you do? Or honestly, have you just broken a nail?

8

SHANNON WAS TEMPTED. How nice it would be to pour out all of her insecurities and confusion onto this unexpectedly broad, masculine shoulder. Where had the geek gone hiding? She looked into Hal's deep blue eyes and saw kindness and compassion there, in spite of the fact that he was annoyed with her.

But no way was she going to talk to this guy. She hadn't even known him twenty-four hours! She looked at her watch to see that it was 7:00 p.m. She'd known him for only *six* hours.

Basically, she'd shaken the man's hand, chopped off his hair and stuck plastic into his eyes. Then she'd jumped his bones. *Smooth, Shan. Real smooth.*

She hadn't even had a meal with him....

"Talk to me," Hal prompted. "You're obviously upset and there has to be a reason."

Shannon ran her fingers over her hair and flashed him a bright smile. "Thanks, Hal. But we don't know each other that well, so—"

"We now know each other intimately," he said.

"But not well."

"Fine. I won't push you. But I'm here if you need to talk."

She had to get things back on a professional footing, if that was even possible now. She kept her toothpaste-commercial smile pasted on. "Thank you."

A long, awkward pause ensued.

"Well," she said with all the perkiness she could muster, "back to business! I'd like you to consider a couple more cosmetic procedures, just to ensure you look your best in photos and on television, okay?"

Hal just stared at her.

"I'd like to take some stray hairs out of your brow line and also have you do a minor bleaching process on your teeth. They're straight, they're even and you've got a great smile, but I'm guessing you drink a lot of coffee?"

Hal put his hands on his hips. "How do you go from your emotional issues to my teeth within thirty seconds like that?"

"Hon, I'm a blonde, remember? So as far as you're concerned, I really don't have emotional issues—just boobs." She made no effort to keep the sarcasm out of her tone. "And disregarding what just happened here, I'm paid to do my job. Shallow as it may be, your eyebrows and your teeth are of critical importance to that job."

"Critical," Hal finally agreed, heavy on the irony.

"Now, on the bright side, you have no unattractive back hair, so we won't be forced to wax that."

"Gosh. That is excellent news."

"But you look like you haven't seen the sun in two decades, so I'm going to get a package for you at a tanning salon."

He glowered at her. "Is that absolutely necessary?"

"Yes. You're a successful president and CEO. You must look as if you play golf and take expensive, glamorous vacations."

"Why? I don't. No time for them."

"Regardless, you've got to look as if you do."

"Fine," Hal sighed. "So next week you're going to bleach my teeth, pluck me and then roast me like a chicken on a spit. I can't wait."

"I also need to get you started at a gym and see your closet," Shannon said decisively. "And we'll need to go shopping."

"Shopping?" Hal blanched. "Shop is a four-letter word. You sure we can't just talk about those emotional issues? Because I think you might be taking out your frustrations on an innocent man, here…."

She ignored him, writing everything down on a notepad. "We're not going to wait until next week on the teeth or the tanning, Hal. You're going to pick up a package of whitening strips at the local pharmacy, and you're going to start at Betsy's 'Burban Beach tomorrow. Just a tip—take *everything* off. You don't want tan lines."

"Everything?" Hal swallowed.

She nodded and kept writing.

"But what if my, uh, rocket gets scorched?"

She looked up at him. He was serious. "Hal. You can cover that with your hands."

"You want me to grip myself in a lighted coffin for twenty minutes?" He was outraged.

"If that bothers you, then wear a sock."

"Unbelievable," he muttered.

"Can I come and look at your closet tomorrow afternoon?"

"Do I have a choice?"

"Nope, not really." She flashed him a cheerfully malicious smile.

"Then tomorrow afternoon would be lovely, Miss Shane. Your wish is my command."

"Now you're talking," she said.

SHANNON'S RIGHT BOOT squished into the wet car carpet every time she shifted the beemer's gears on the way to Hal's house. The whole vehicle smelled musty, and it was her own damn fault. She doubted the leather seats would ever recover from the soaking they'd gotten yesterday, during her wild drive in the rain. *Stupid, stupid, stupid.* What got into her sometimes? She honestly didn't know. But it hadn't seemed right that the rest of Farmington should go on existing peacefully when her whole world had been kicked off-kilter by her mother's revelation. She'd needed to shake up the place, snap herself out of her daze, shock a few placid souls on their way to the ATM or the supermarket or the elementary school. Judging by the stares sent her way, she'd accomplished her goal.

To the detriment of her car, this car that seemed all wrong for her. Too expensive, too shiny, too exclusive, too status-conscious. Was that the kind of person she'd grown into? Or did the car just represent the best of German engineering, natural elegance and quality?

She heard the wet squish again as she downshifted, exiting the highway to get to Hal's house in Simsbury, a town of quiet charm about twenty minutes from Hartford proper.

She passed the town hall on the right and a large cemetery to the left, with gravestones as far as the eye could see. All of those people, she thought, had once been alive and productive and loved by their families. They'd all had identities of their own, knew their niches in the grand scheme of things, unlike her.

A stocky mother waited to cross Main Street with her daughter, the child looking up at her with adoration. Shannon swallowed a lump in her throat that had appeared uninvited. The little girl had no worldly knowledge, but she knew where she came from, knew whose lives intertwined hers. She was young enough still to be blessed with unconditional love.

Shannon shrugged off the unwelcome thoughts invading her mind. Three more quick turns had her driving down Hal's street to a surprisingly modern house. There weren't many contemporary homes in the area, New England being a bastion of the traditional and the quaint.

Two last squishes in the beemer's carpet and

she was on the sidewalk, striding toward Hal's domain. The place was stucco, also unusual, and he'd painted his front door cerulean blue. Next to it a single, scraggly-looking holly bush reached courageously for the sun. She wished it luck and good fertilizer before ringing the bell.

Hal opened it almost immediately and gestured her in.

"Hi," she said, struck again by the strength of his jaw and the intense blue of his eyes. Now, she'd have to get him to stand straight instead of slouching, dress him decently and drag him to that gym.

Whew. They only had a few short weeks. And during that time she had to coach him for the media, too. She foresaw many hours in each other's company.

"Hi, Shannon. Are you feeling happier today?" He looked at her searchingly.

The question caught her off guard. "Uh. Yes, thank you."

"Hmm." He didn't seem to believe her.

"Really," she said with a bright smile. "Everything's fine." She looked past him at the foyer and the living room beyond. She'd never seen a house so bare. The foyer contained a single black umbrella and an empty coatrack, nothing else. No mirror or rug or pictures on the walls.

The living room, too, was all bachelor and function—no creature comforts besides a massive, over-stuffed, cotton-duck sofa, an elaborate state-of-the-art entertainment center, and what looked like a bouquet of remote controls radiating from a simple glass bowl on an elliptical steel coffee table. No art hung on the walls, though a stack of framed pictures, protected by cardboard corner covers, leaned into a corner. Shannon's guess was that they'd been delivered by his mother or sister—a well-meaning female in his life—and he'd promptly forgotten them.

"So…what's that in your purse?" Hal eyed the black plastic hanging out of it.

She cleared her throat. "That's a lawn-and-leaf bag."

He blinked.

She smiled reassuringly. "You know, in case we need to weed some stuff out of your closet." She thought it best not to mention that most of his clothes would likely need burning. It didn't seem kind. Though if his closet was as minimal as the house, she wouldn't have much to do.

"Oh." They stood in awkward silence for a moment. He seemed fascinated by her hair. She really, *really* shouldn't have had sex with him.

Shannon dropped her hobo bag, twisted the mass of hair behind her head and secured it with a pencil, true to habit. "Well, do you want to show me where your bedroom is?" The question sounded odd and intimate to her own ears.

"Yeah." Hal turned and led the way out of the foyer. The first article of clothing she'd need to burn was the pair of jeans he had on. They fit poorly and were more fray than hem at the bottom. She was a big fan of faded denim on men, but it had to be made

by Levi's only and hug the buns properly. She pon-
dered how to get them off him so she could toss them
into her Hefty bag. Hot seduction, take two?

Hal had a big, rangy frame. Any essence of nerd
he possessed came from the way he carried himself,
not his actual build. He was completely unassuming,
as if he'd just been too busy to notice when God had
filled out his shoulders and broadened his chest.
Shannon, used to the buff, gym-trained bodies of
L.A., found it endearing. Somehow it made her want
to hug him.

He led the way down a hall to the master bedroom,
which was surprisingly orderly, except for a crop of
dirty socks dropped at the end of the bed. *Men.* Why
they considered it impossible to walk them to a laundry basket, she'd never know. Her last, brief boyfriend, Brian, had done the same thing, waiting for
the socks to skip by themselves into the washer. The
only difference was he'd thrown them to the left side
of his bed, not the foot.

Looking at Hal's bed made her oddly self-con-
scious; aware that she was standing in the private space
of someone she didn't know very well, even if they'd
been *intimate,* as he put it. He had squashy goose-down
pillows, her favorite, and a fluffy down-filled duvet.

She knew a crazy urge to be ten again, and take a
flying leap from the doorway into the center of the mat-
tress. Funny, that—she usually tensed up in a man's
bedroom, wondering when he would pounce on her
and expect her to fulfill his every pin-up girl fantasy.

Hal moved to the double closet doors and pulled them open. Inside minimalism had died a horrible death, buried under an avalanche of dated and hideous clothing.

Shannon stared at it in disbelief. Was that a plaid Western shirt with pearlized snaps? Ye gods. And a color-block shirt from the eighties. And a red-and-blue argyle vest…then there were a couple of dated eighties suits, in tan and light blue, made of fabrics she wouldn't even use for drop cloths.

"Hal? Have you ever gone through and purged your closet completely?"

"Well, I've gotten rid of things that didn't fit." He seemed pleased with that.

She turned to him with a fixed smile. "I see. Listen. I see a lot of things here that…well, they won't quite work with the new image we're going for. The *GQ*, media-ready Hal Underwood. You're becoming a power player, so we'll need to get you power clothes."

"Power clothes," he repeated doubtfully.

"Yes."

"How much is this going to cost me?"

She decided to sidestep that particular issue. "I'm not sure yet. But will you trust me to get rid of what needs to go? I mean, I know you've got a ton of work to do." She flashed him a winning smile.

His eyes narrowed. "Yeah, but I think I'll just get my laptop and do it right in here."

Damn. The battle commences. Shannon rolled up

her sleeves. By the time he'd returned with his lap-top, she had a third of his closet on the floor in heaps.

It was bloody war. He fought for every shirt she pulled out, every ratty pair of jeans, and even shoes that were curled at the toes and blue-green with mold, or had barely any leather left to them.

"Those can be resoled!" he insisted.

"Veto."

"Carpenter bell-bottoms are still fine for mowing the lawn…"

"Yeah, no. What a shame—the zipper's broken."

"I saw you twist it! What the hell…?" He grabbed for the denim, but Shannon stuffed the jeans into the bag and sat on it. She looked up and blinked her eyes, all innocence.

"I did no such thing." She tugged at a hideous ma-roon velour jacket next.

"Velour is fine for inside the house."

"No, velour is not fine for *anything* on a man. Erase the concept of it from your mind. Toss!"

"But—hey! No way! That Western snap shirt is a souvenir from Texas."

She shuddered. "Maybe so, but you'll get arrested if you wear it in Connecticut." She ripped a sicken-ing checked jacket from its hanger and rubbed her eyes to see if it would go away. Nope.

"I paid seventy bucks for that blazer," Hal moaned, "and it still almost buttons."

"Key word—*almost.* We won't discuss the fact that it's unlined." She shoved it into the bag.

"Hey, I didn't agree—"

"Hal, honey. I wouldn't use that horrifying rag to clean my toilet. Let it go."

When they got finished, a total of seven items were left in Hal's closet, and he looked stricken. "Three white shirts," he moaned. "Two pairs of jeans…one tie and a windbreaker? That's all you're leaving me?"

"Yup." Shannon, merciless, finished tying a knot in the third lawn-and-leaf bag. She turned to him with an evil grin. "And, babe, that's only so you won't go naked to work while I start to build your new wardrobe."

"You…you give new meaning to the word brutality," he complained.

"I know," she agreed. "I realize this is traumatic for you. But really, it's for the best. You just wait. The reincarnated Hal will be beating off women with a stick."

"But I don't like pushy women."

"Then you sure must not like me much!" She flashed another grin at him.

"Not true," he said seriously. "I like you a lot. Even though you're a fashion bully."

"Well, thanks, Hal. I like you, too." She touched his arm. The muscle jumped under her fingers. "You've been a pretty good sport about this."

He moved away. "I didn't expect to like you," he said suddenly.

She sucked in a quick breath. "Why?"

"You're too…gorgeous…to be nice."

9

HE MAY AS WELL have slapped her. Shannon stared at him for a long moment before she grabbed one of the overstuffed black bags and started pulling it toward his bedroom door. The same old issues followed her wherever she went, it seemed.

I swear to God I'm going to get a prescription for Rogaine and use it to grow a mustache. I'm going to eat fried food and chocolate until nobody sees me under the fat.

She sighed. Who was she kidding? She was just as much caught in the trap as anybody else, trained from birth to cultivate her looks for attention.

"Hey," Hal called after her. "I didn't mean that the way it sounded. And let me take that, it's too heavy for you."

She ignored him and continued to drag the bag, pulling it along his hardwood floors with a *whoosh*. She was upset enough about his comment that she dropped all pretense of professional demeanor.

"A lot of people assume that I can't be a nice person, and I hate it. Do you know how few close friends

I have? Two. I have two—my business partners, Jane and Lilia, whom I've known since we were all eight, with snaggleteeth and braids. Other than that I have hundreds of acquaintances."

"Shannon—"

"I feel eyes boring into me everywhere I go, measuring, assessing, comparing."

"I never thought about that."

"Why is it that because I look a certain way—" she turned and asked the question quietly, without heat "—everyone assumes that I'm deficient in every other department? That I'm stuck-up, or stupid, or shallow or useless?"

"They're jealous," he told her. "That's all."

She dropped the bag and put her hands on her hips, breathing fast. "You're not jealous! Unless you're telling me that you're a closet drag queen. But you just judged me the same way."

"I didn't," he insisted. "I'm wary, that's all. Your looks are…intimidating. You seem like a being from some Planet of Perfection, where there are no flaws."

"Planet of…?" Speechless, she let her hands drop to her sides. "That's nuts. Look, I have huge feet, and a big ugly mottled birthmark on my thigh, and flabby upper arms. I go to the bathroom, same as everybody else. I'm not manufactured by Mattel!"

"Hey," said Hal. "Calm down." He put a soothing hand between her shoulder blades and rubbed. Normally she hated being touched, but he did it to comfort, to relax, and not to grab or own. She didn't move away.

"Sorry," she said. "I don't mean to take out my issues on you, of all people. You're my client."

"It's been a long afternoon. Would you like a beer? I wish I had wine to offer, but…"

"I'd love a beer, thanks."

Hal went to the stainless steel refrigerator in the kitchen and she followed. It was the cleanest kitchen she'd ever seen: obviously unused.

"You don't cook much, do you?"

"Nope." He handed her a cold green bottle after twisting the cap off.

"Thank you. Did you just move into this place?" She took a sip and felt the pleasantly bitter bubbles spread over her tongue before heading down her throat.

He nodded. "About a month ago. My accountant kept nagging me about how I was pouring money down the drain by renting, and how I needed the tax write-off from a house." He put his own bottle to his lips and she noticed again how beautifully shaped they were. They formed an ironic quirk in his face, saved his blue eyes from being angelic. Hal might not be a sophisticated man-about-town, but she knew that he was no angel. Angels didn't make love the way he did. Have sex. Whatever.

She took a swig of beer to distract herself from that train of thought, because she was starting to want to jump him again.

"So I obviously struck a nerve," Hal ventured.

She began to peel the label off her beer bottle. "Yeah."

"Sorry. I guess we all carry around our pasts and the ideas we form from them. Most of the really pretty girls in my past were stuck-up. They knew they were beautiful and they used it. Unfortunately you remind me of one of them."

"And she wasn't nice?"

He raised his own beer bottle to his lips and drank from it. "Definitely not."

"To you in particular?"

"Yeah."

"What did she do?"

"You really want to know?"

Shannon nodded.

"Samantha Stanton. That was her name. Gorgeous. She used to wheedle my trig homework out of me and copy it before class. Stupid me, I let her. Then she wanted me to pass her test answers and I wouldn't play ball. So Sam got even.

"Around prom time she lied and said she'd broken up with her boyfriend—would I take her? Part of me was suspicious. I mean, why would a varsity cheerleader want the chess club nerd to take her to prom? But another part of me, probably my dick, believed her.

"So I rented a cheesy tux and shiny plastic shoes, slicked my hair back and bought a corsage. Showed up on her doorstep."

He stopped and shook his head. Took another swig of beer.

Shannon waited.

"The front door of her palatial home opens, and it's a whole preparty. Half the football team, her boyfriend, all of her snotty girlfriends and cheerleader buddies. And they all fall down laughing at me, the dork on the doorstep who thought he had a chance in hell of taking Samantha to the prom."

Shannon sucked in her breath in horror.

"I was so humiliated I could barely breathe."

"What did you do?"

Hal shrugged. "I left. I thought about putting sugar in her gas tank. I thought about a lot of things. Used to dream about revenge…especially when the crank calls came late at night. She and her friends used to think it was funny to talk dirty to me. Get the nerd all hot and bothered and hang up on him. I guess the idea was to leave me with a big boner for their entertainment. Nice, huh? Those were the days before caller ID."

"I'm so glad I remind you of this girl. Sheesh."

"Actually, Sam's not such a looker anymore." Hal grinned. "I didn't actually attend my high school reunion, but I hear she's now the size of a whale, has three horrific kids by her high school boyfriend and he's a deadbeat drunk."

"What goes around comes around," said Shannon.

"Seems like it," he agreed.

They sat in companionable silence for a few minutes. Then she said, "Hal…I don't want you to think I normally have sex with people after knowing them six hours."

"What, you like to know them at least eight?" His tone was teasing, but his glance was sharp and evaluative.

"At least." She played along and was flip. "No, really. I'm pretty picky. But I had some upsetting news the other day—no, I still don't want to talk about it—and then I just felt this spark with you, and all of a sudden it seemed right and natural and…and…urgent."

"Urgent?"

"Yeah. The connection part. I wasn't just horny—though of course that was part of it—I needed to reach something in you. Something rare and elusive that you have. Though I can't say I know what it is." She peeled off the rest of the label.

Then she stared him straight in the eyes. "I might have started off using you for comfort sex. But it didn't end that way. I want you to know that."

HAL HAD HEARD pretty speeches before. He gave them about as much credence as he did pretty women. Maybe this one was nice, but she was obviously letting him down easy. She was saying, "Don't think you're going to get lucky again," while at the same time trying to make him believe that the encounter was more than it was.

She was throwing him a bone.

Some things never changed. There were goddesses and there were dorks. He might be a dork with money and prospects now, but he was still a dork.

"Did you hear me?" Shannon asked.

He realized that he'd been off in mental space and hadn't responded. "Uh. Yeah. Thanks."

"Thanks?" She seemed taken aback.

He nodded.

"What are you…can I ask what you're thinking?"

You can ask. "Oh, I'm just preoccupied." *True.* "About an information leak in my company. I'm worried about it, and whether it will affect the IPO. And it pisses me off that I can't find the source. I don't know where it's coming from."

"Is someone hacking in?"

"They'd have to be really, really good to get by my security. I'm not saying it's impossible, but it's unlikely. And I can't find a trace of the hacker."

"Could it be a corporate spy? Someone on the inside?"

Hal thought about it. Was Declan the culprit? No. The taciturn Irishman was honest to a fault. He filled out time sheets to the minute. Was it Trent, his marketing guy? Doubtful. Trent wanted to protect his job and his stock holdings in the company. He'd have no reason to betray Hal, since he'd be sitting pretty after the IPO.

Again, Hal's thoughts turned to Ryan. He hated to think that someone he knew and liked and trusted would sell him out. Ryan didn't really have a motive…except for envy, perhaps. A couple of years ago, he'd been part of a business venture that had gone belly-up. He'd lost a lot of capital.

Ryan knew more than the average attorney about

computers. He had a key to Hal's offices. He'd had the access.

Hal pushed the thought away. Ryan was his best friend. He wouldn't sabotage Underwood Technologies. Would he?

"Well," Shannon said. "I can't say that I know much about corporate theft. I can tell you what a spy should *wear,* but not how he would go about his business." She shrugged.

Hal blinked at her. "What a spy should *wear?* You're kidding, right?"

"Yes, I'm kidding. Is anybody lurking around your office in the stereotypical trench coat, black turtleneck and dark glasses?"

He laughed. "Now that you mention it, my receptionist, Tina, does own a shiny pink raincoat. She favors low-cut tops instead of turtlenecks, though."

"There you go. It's obviously Tina." Shannon smiled. "Now that I've solved your mystery, I'd better be off to Goodwill with my lawn-and-leaf bags."

"*My* lawn-and-leaf bags," Hal grumbled.

"Nope. Mine. I brought them, remember?"

"Yeah, but my entire closet's in those! And you're about to give them away."

"Not your whole closet," said Shannon, eyeing the jeans he wore in a highly suspect way. "Just most of it."

Was it his imagination, or were her fingers twitching? She reminded him of a tiger, circling her prey.

"You cannot have my pants," he said.

"Mwah ha ha ha."

"No! This is my favorite pair of jeans and you're not getting them off my body."

Shannon rubbed her hands together evilly. She raised an eyebrow. "What if I made it worth your while?"

"What do you mean by that?"

"What would you like me to mean?"

Was she offering him sex if he took his pants off for her? His cock twitched at the thought. "Well, a guy can always fantasize," he said, before he could stop himself.

"So can a girl," she purred. "But the reality is so much more satisfying, don't you think?" And she whipped off her top.

She is not doing this. I have died and gone to heaven. I have met a crazy blond nympho with a taste for nerds!

Hal sprung a woody in two seconds flat. He wet his lips as his torturess unsnapped her bra and her truly magnificent breasts fell free.

"I figure we've known each other for twenty-eight hours now," Shannon said, "so we've gotten acquainted."

"Whatever you say," Hal agreed. Her pink, sultry nipples had wide aureoles that just begged for his mouth. They hardened under his gaze and he wanted to suck them until she cried out for mercy.

He wanted to rip off her remaining clothes and set her hot little ass on the ceramic cooktop, where he'd bring her to a fast boil and then stir her up all over again. Then he wanted her thighs pressing against his ears as she called his name and he tasted her, rolled her on his tongue like vintage wine, and swallowed her essence.

Hal was so hard now that he figured he was in danger of drilling a hole right through his pants. He set his beer down and moved purposefully toward her, removing his own shirt.

She'd unfastened the button to her jeans and slid them down her lean hips. She stepped out of one leg of the pants but he reached her and bent his head to her lips before she got the other foot out.

Shannon swayed into him, her breasts brushing against his chest hair, and it drove him wild. He licked into her mouth and devoured her, cupping her breasts and running his thumbs over her nipples at the same time. She moaned.

Through the fog of utter lust, he still couldn't quite believe that this goddess was giving herself to him again. He bent her back in his arms and took her left breast into his mouth, sucking hard and insistently, communicating his desire with every pull. He pinched the right nipple, then caressed the smooth globe surrounding it before switching his attentions to that breast.

He worked his knee between hers and brought it up to the juncture of her thighs, where she was hot and wet through her panties. She pressed against it and writhed, turning him on even more.

She reached out and cupped his cock through the jeans while he groaned. "Off," she said. "Take them off so I can feel you in my hands."

He ditched them in record time, along with his boxers, and felt her hands caress the length of him, squeeze him at the root, rub her fingers along the sensitive, engorged underside. He was afraid he'd lose control and come right then.

Hal took her hands away, over her murmur of protest, lifted her bodily so that her knees went around his waist and drove into her, helpless with lust. She was tight and hot and deliciously, sinfully wet. He contracted with sheer pleasure, shaking with the force of it.

She was making unintelligible noises, her fingernails digging into his shoulders, her mouth open and plump and willing. He pulled out a few inches and drove back in, panting with physical exertion and restraint. He wanted to draw it out, make it good for her, even though every nerve in his body screamed for a primal, uncivilized pounding.

Hal wanted to screw her into next week, next month, next year. The suction and muscular stroking of her inner walls on his erection was finally too much. He was going to either come or pull out. Gritting his teeth, cursing under his breath, wanting to stay in so badly that his decision was actively painful, he withdrew.

"No," she panted. "Please."

"I want this to be good for you."

"It couldn't possibly be better…."

Hal turned her back to him so that he could have full access to her breasts while inside her. They took two steps and he bent her over his granite kitchen counter. He smoothed his hands over her backside, found her lower lips again and drove solidly, thickly between them while she gasped and almost sobbed.

Then he took her breasts in each hand and began to slowly torture and tease her nipples again as he moved his penis in and out, in and out, in and out. Her breath became ragged and she whimpered, cried out, then convulsed around him.

The sight of her climax, her no-holds-barred pleasure, made him come, too. He buried himself to the hilt and let the waves of sensation pull him into ecstasy.

10

SHANNON VAGUELY became aware of reality. The cold granite pressed against her breasts, and her hot client pressed against her backside, his arms encircling her and his big hands covering her own. He kissed the top of her head.

"Woman," said Hal, "you're going to kill me." He backed off her and dropped to the floor, panting.

She turned and pushed the hair out of her face, still breathless herself, still humming with the rush of sensation. Unfortunately that faded fast and left her just naked and vulnerable and embarrassed by her complete response to him. What happened to her cool around this guy? And she was supposed to be teaching it to *him*.

Cool, hip, image-conscious people didn't bite and claw, whimper or moan or scream with delirious pleasure.

God sure must get a good laugh when He looks down and sees human beings having sex. Shannon found her panties and pulled them on, wincing at that bird's-eye visual.

Well, at least they'd used his kitchen for something. And she'd gotten those terrible jeans off him.

"Damn, but you're beautiful." Hal lay spread-eagle, still half-erect, and stared up at her. "I could get used to this."

Warning bells went off in her head. She'd heard those words before. Truth to tell, she'd heard them many times. Another man, responding to her sexually but not really in any other way.

She forced a smile, though. And a little laugh. She found her bra.

"Wait," Hal said. "Is it strictly necessary for you to put your clothes back on?" He waggled his eyebrows and pulled himself upright. "I've gone from boner to temporarily boneless...but I'll recover soon."

She laughed again, as expected. *Just like a man.* The guy wanted *more* sex. She needed distance.

On the one hand, it was nice to be sexually attractive to him. On the other, she was desperate to be seen and desired for herself, and not her face, legs and breasts.

Hal staggered toward a half bathroom near the kitchen. "I'll be back."

"Okay." She stared after him and then caught sight of herself in the reflection of the microwave. She was standing butt naked in her client's kitchen after screwing his brains out. Her reflection was squat and distorted, so that she looked like a squished, chubby, blond troll.

As the water went on in the bathroom, and her

emotions continued to swirl and conflict, she made a quick, unconscious decision to get the hell out of there. She jumped into her clothes, opened the door, grabbed her purse. She remembered the lawn-and-leaf bags and dragged them out after her.

She cast a paranoid glance back at the kitchen to see if Hal had emerged yet, and saw those awful jeans of his lying on the floor. This was probably her only chance.... Shannon hesitated. Then she stole them and ran.

HAL WAS UTTERLY unprepared for the reactions of his co-workers on Monday morning to the New Him.

He was still mystified by Shannon's behavior and outraged at the loss of his favorite jeans, but Hal was trying to turn over a new, cool leaf.

So instead of just slouching by with his nose in his coffee, he said hello to the bent, brunette head of Tina, his receptionist, as he bypassed her on the way to his office.

"Hey..." she muttered back, from inside a file drawer. "Uh, you've got several messages already. Your mom, a reporter from—" She broke into silence. "*Hal? Is that you?* Oh, my God!"

"What?"

"Your hair! Your...face. We can *see* it. Wow. You look...amazing."

He shifted from one foot to the other in his ancient, dirty gym shoes, pleased despite himself. "I do?"

"Yeah. Wait, come 'ere, lemme get the piece of tissue off your chin. Spoils the effect." Tina emerged from behind her desk. She wore business attire, but as usual it appeared sprayed on. Her blouse was cut so low it was a millimeter from indecent, and her navy skirt clung to her behind like a surgical glove. She was also in her stocking feet, since she habitually wore painful shoes.

Hal didn't care if she was barefoot, as long as she answered his phone and kept him organized.

"Oh, that. I cut myself shaving this morning. I'm not used to it." What he didn't add was that it was a damned nuisance to have to shave every morning. Much easier to roll out of bed, into the shower and out the door without bothering.

"Where are your glasses?" Tina asked as she stared up at him and pulled off the tissue. Was it his imagination, or had she come closer than necessary?

"Well, uh. This image consultant woman I saw over the weekend—she didn't seem to like them too much." Speaking of her, Hal frowned. The naked blond thief! Somebody was probably paying ten bucks for his jeans right now. Unless he could make a run over to Goodwill and snag them back?

"You don't say." Tina snapped her gum and blinked her big dark eyes with a little too much innocence. "So you got contacts?"

He nodded. "Yup. These soft ones are really comfortable. You can sleep in them! I never knew. And we ordered a new pair of glasses from some snooty designer in Los Angeles…" He took the corner of tissue from Tina's fingers. "I'll throw that away, thanks."

Her gaze had shifted down to his attire, frayed baggy jeans and a grayish T-shirt under an open, white, long-sleeved button-down. "Is this, uh, image lady going to take you shopping?"

"Unfortunately, yes." He rubbed his hand protectively over the gray T-shirt. Miss Evil hadn't dumped out his laundry hamper, thank God.

"Good." Tina nodded. "Listen to her. She obviously knows what she's doing."

Hal barely restrained a snort. "What did my mother want? And you mentioned a reporter?"

"Your mom wants you to come to her open-mike poetry reading at some club."

Hal groaned.

"And the reporter is with *Business Today.* Get this, they wanna do a feature on you and Underwood Tech! Isn't that fab?"

He nodded. *As long as I can track down this information leak, it's fab.* "Uh, when?"

"The guy wants to see you next Thursday if you can fit him in. Says he needs about two hours of your time."

Ugh. Sounded like a lot of small talk. And he'd need to be careful about what to reveal and what was off-limits because of the IPO. What the hell did you wear to meet with a reporter? This was all new territory for him. He'd have to ask Shannon—though he wasn't sure he was speaking to the woman.

"Oh," Tina added, "I need you to sign these forms here and here—" she pointed "—and then Ryan needs to get with you on a contract before the ten-thirty meeting, and don't forget that two o'clock conference call with All-Nation."

Of course…then there were the server issues to deal with, a couple of test runs on programs, and more. Another day, another dollar. He headed for his office, Tina's forms in hand.

"Hal?" she called after him.

"Yes?"

"Come 'ere again."

What now?

"Bend your head down, you're too tall—"

He knit his brows in question, but did as she asked.

"There!" She'd pulled something out of his newly short hair, a glob of gel. Yuck. Hal flushed, embarrassed, as she wiped it on a paper towel.

"Honey, didn't the girl at the salon teach you to rub it all over your hands like lotion? *Then* you smooth it onto your head." Tina chuckled.

"Oh. I'm not too good at this fashion stuff yet." He thought about Enrique's purplish face, mottled with rage when he'd left the royal premises. He hadn't given any instructions with the plastic jar of crud he'd tossed after them.

"Thanks, Tina."

"No problem. Your next project should be getting some pants that fit. You look completely buttless in those."

Buttless? Great. Hal sidestepped the question of why, all of a sudden, his receptionist was checking out his rear view. He went to go find Ryan instead.

SHANNON STARED at the phone in her office and then at Hal's work number. She had to call him in order to do her job and take him shopping. There was no other way around it.

"Hey, Shan?" Jane's voice traveled from the reception area. "Do you have any idea why the leg on this desk is cracked? Almost like someone heavy sat on it. And it's sort of pushed to the side."

Yikes. "Oh, you're kidding!" Shan exclaimed, injecting her voice with just the right amount of surprise. "No, I don't have the slightest idea."

"I swear that this looks like a...*butt-print.* Ugh! It *is* a butt-print! What has the cleaning staff been up to in here? It's bad enough that the desk was dusty, but *this?*"

Shannon thought fast. "Well, that explains why my radio was tuned to a country-and-western station."

Jane was outraged. "I'm calling the janitorial service right now to complain!"

Shannon felt lower than a worm. Because of her, some innocent person was going to get in trouble— possibly even fired. "Jane, hon, why don't you let me call—I've lost an earring, too, and I'll ask them whether anyone found it."

Her partner cocked an eyebrow. "You have four hundred pairs of earrings. Why would you miss one?"

"They're my favorite," Shan lied. "You know, the ones with the peridots and amethysts?"

Jane seemed to halfway buy it. "Fine. I'll get you the number. But I want to know what the manager says." She walked into Shan's office brandishing a Rolodex card and hovered, waiting for her to make the call.

Great. Shannon inhaled a breath and punched in Hal's direct line instead. If she faked a number then Jane would hear the electronic operator's voice.

He answered in two rings. "Hal Underwood."

"Mr. Munson," she said cordially. "This is Shannon Shane, with Finesse. How are you?"

"I want my pants back," growled Hal. "And who the hell is Mr. Munson? Did you steal his pants, too?"

"Well, I'm fine, thanks. But I do have a small matter to discuss with you, if you have a moment."

"Nice of you to say goodbye."

"Yes. Well, it seems that one of your staff sat on our Queen Anne reception desk while cleaning over the weekend, Mr. Munson. Can you explain that?"

"Yeah, a blond nymphomaniac attacked me in my truck, yanked me into her place of business and jumped me on the reception desk."

"I am *not* a— No, I'm afraid it couldn't have been anyone else."

"After knowing me six hours."

Hey! She'd done her best to explain that. "Well, we do have some physical evidence, Mr. Munson. But we'd rather not have to take that to court. We'd rather just settle this in a civilized way. And next time you can send us a different cleaning team, okay?"

"Physical evidence?" asked Hal, who sounded like he was taking a sip of his coffee.

"Yes. It's a...well, Mr. Munson, I don't quite know how to phrase this. It's a, uh, a butt-print."

Hal clearly spit something on the other end of the line.

"Mr. Munson? Are you okay?"

"Is it your butt-print or mine? It has to be yours... That's very funny, you know. What's the matter, is your partner standing right there while you pretend to call the cleaning service?"

"Thank you, Mr. Munson. We would appreciate that. Yes, cash is fine. You have a good week, too." Shannon hung up and looked calmly at Jane. "All taken care of. I'll go pick up the money from him."

"Great." Jane turned and left her office. Then she called over her shoulder. "Oh, but Shannon. You forgot to ask about your earring. And Mr. Munson didn't seem to ask the price of the desk. Plus, even if he had, I doubt it was his cleaning staff that left the five long, curly, blond hairs caught under the lamp."

Shannon winced.

"So you get to disinfect every inch of that desk, Shane, and then polish it with lemon oil. You also get to call a furniture repair place and have the leg fixed or replaced."

Jane stuck her head back into Shannon's office, her expression cheerfully malicious. "And honey, we own a business called Finesse. Remember? I don't think making butt-prints in Reception falls under that heading."

Shannon shot the finger at her.

"That doesn't qualify, either. Now are you going to tell me about this mystery man?"

Shannon shook her head.

"Didn't think so." Jane gave a resigned shrug of the shoulders and finally left her in peace.

Shannon stared at her phone again, smacked herself in the forehead and hit Redial.

11

"OPERATION SHOPPING begins at 4:00 p.m. sharp," Shannon said when Hal answered.

"You again!"

"Sorry about the Mr. Munson thing. Yes, Jane was standing over me."

"Can I have a copy of the butt-print as a memento of you?"

"No. And why would you need a memento of me?"

"You know. A keepsake. So I can look back fondly on the day that the goddess took pity on the nerd and did him out of mercy."

Speechless, Shannon just stared at the phone.

"Hello?"

She recovered. "Just what the hell is that supposed to mean? Are you still living in some high school fantasy?"

"Aw, I was kidding."

"I don't think so. And you are not a nerd. You just need a little polish, which is why I'm taking you shopping this afternoon."

Hal groaned. "Is there any way that I can just pay you extra to go without me? I could try on the stuff later…"

"Nice try at sliming out of this, but it won't work. We don't have time to waste on me making endless returns. Oh, and by the way, we have a personal training session at the gym at eight o'clock."

"I have things to do. I have a company to run. I can't just leave at four and not come back!"

"How long until that IPO? How long until your first media interview?"

"Okay, okay."

"I'll pick you up in the moldy beemer at your office."

"You didn't have the carpet professionally cleaned and dried?" Hal's tone was scandalized.

"Nope."

TODAY SHE WAS WEARING silver leather pants, red spike-heeled boots and a body-hugging red sweater. Her handbag looked like a work of art out of a museum.

Hal stared at it as he climbed gingerly into Shannon's car. He wondered how much it had cost and decided he probably didn't want to know. He had a bad, bad feeling about the kinds of shops a woman like her frequented. How much poorer would he be at the end of the day?

They drove for an hour and a half until they got to Hal's worst nightmare: a gigantic shopping mall in the suburbs of New York. The Westchester sported both a Neiman Marcus and a Saks and he'd also spied a big Bloomingdale's around the corner. His male heart sank into the treads of his running shoes.

Apparently they were going into Neiman's first, since she parked close to it. Hal stared balefully at the entrance before girding his loins and getting out of the car, which stank of mildew.

He shoved his hands into his pockets while Shannon locked the beemer and threw the keys into her work-of-art bag. In her designer sunglasses and the beautiful leather pants, she looked like a Bond girl about to go somewhere on 007's arm. She took his, instead.

"Hal, where did you get those clothes? I know exactly what I left in your closet and those weren't there."

His chest swelled with manly pride. "You never checked my laundry hamper."

She put a hand to her temple. "You're wearing dirty stuff?"

"No. I washed them."

"Well, that's something, then. We can donate them on the way out of here."

"I like these pants. I like this T-shirt. They're comfortable. You're not giving them away. And I want my other jeans back, you thief! That was really low."

"Sometimes I have to resort to desperate measures to get my job done." She looked at him over the top of her glasses. "And I'm happy to say that the other jeans are long gone."

"Could you at least show the tiniest bit of remorse? Could you fake it?"

"No. You looked like an abandoned scarecrow in those. And those shoes..." Words seemed to fail her. She tugged him into the department store and propelled him into the men's shoe department.

"Hello," she said sweetly to a wizened little salesman. "This gentleman needs footwear. Badly. And if you have a metal trash can and a lighter, that would be excellent. I have hairspray in my purse."

"Hairspray, madam?"

"Flammable," she explained. "I'll drench those horrors he has on his feet."

"Madam, the Neiman Marcus fire code does not permit—"

"No?" she asked in sorrowful tones. "Well, then I'll just have to toss them in the Dumpster. Not nearly as much fun, though."

"Great," Hal muttered into her ear. "So you're a pyromaniac as well as a nymphomaniac."

"Hal, honey, when will you understand that I'm just a maniac, period? Now sit down." She pushed him into a chair, where he crossed his arms and glared at them.

"I need a loafer in cordovan and one in saddle leather," she said to the salesman.

Hal shot out of his chair. "No penny loafers!"

She nodded but otherwise ignored him. "And a casual lace-up, one black, one brown. Then we'll need dress shoes in black, brown and cordovan. For extremely casual, we'll need a hiking boot and a nice Italian sandal—"

"No way," said Hal.

"Disregard the gentleman, please," she said, adjusting her sunglasses over her long blond hair. "He doesn't understand what he needs." She added under her breath, "And under no circumstances are you to tell him the price of anything."

"Very good, madam. May I offer you two some refreshment?"

"Yeah," said Hal gloomily. "Strong liquor."

"Sir, I deeply regret to inform you that Neiman Marcus is unable to provide you with spirits. Perhaps a glass of wine?"

"Do you have beer?" Hal asked.

"Sir, I deeply regret—"

"To inform me that you have no beer, either. Fine, let's get on with this miserable process."

The little man raised his chin. "Sir, here at Neiman Marcus we strive to provide our customers with the highest level of service. We also attempt to ensure that our clientele *enjoys* their visits to our retail establishment. Under no circumstances do we wish you to feel that your selection process is a miserable experience."

"Then just bring me some shoes," Hal begged.

"Very good, sir." The salesman scuttled off.

"Hal, that was rude. Becoming a cool guy means that you have an easy, relaxed demeanor. You never sweat anything, especially not such a small thing as buying shoes."

He snorted. "Yeah, but I don't think we're just

buying shoes. We're starting to waste my entire life savings on stupidities."

She sighed. "Well, get used to it. Because we've got a lot more 'stupidities' to buy."

HAL STOOD like a coatrack with arms as yet another wizened little man sucked on the pins between his teeth and drew chalk lines on the suit that Hal wore. His new shoes pinched his little toes, which were beginning to go numb. Shannon, relentless in pursuit of his new wardrobe, dove among the clothing displays like a gorgeous bird of prey. Each time she surfaced with yet another jacket or sweater, he blanched. How could women possibly like to shop?

It was torture. Sheer, unmitigated, gruesome torture. And worse, all of this stuff was going to have to be dry-cleaned!

Shannon winged by with a couple of cashmere sweaters that probably cost more than the national debt, and he brought the subject to her attention. "Do you realize how much it's going to cost me to take care of these stupid clothes? Do you know how bad dry-cleaning is for the environment? The fluid also causes cancer!" He quoted several statistics at her until the salesman/tailor stuck him in the ankle with a pin. "Ow!"

"Begging your pardon, sir. We here at Neiman Marcus do strive not to stab the customers, but occasionally we err. We are only human. Would you care for a bandage, sir? Or a complimentary tetanus shot?"

"What?" said Hal. "No!"

"You mean, 'No thanks, man,'" said Shannon.

"Oh, I do, do I?" Hal said in ominous tones.

"Yes. And it's definitely not cool to go around spouting statistics about dry-cleaning fluid. So drop that."

"You may be stunning to look at, but you are starting to piss me off."

"No, no, no." Shannon shook her finger. "You're cool, remember? You don't sweat it."

Hal counted to three and stared at her breasts for a distraction. They were so plump and happy nestled in that red sweater…just the right amount of swoop.

She turned and went back to the racks of clothing, displaying her silver-leather-clad delectable bottom. He stared at that, too. He forgot about how annoying she was and cooked up quite the little fantasy. It involved her naked on a baby-oiled waterbed…

"Sir? Begging your pardon, sir, but I'm having difficulties marking your alterations. We at Neiman Marcus are dedicated to the highest quality of customer service. Given the, er, circumstances, may I provide you with an explicit magazine and a private bathroom?"

Hal looked down and blinked. He sported an enormous, gabardine-clothed erection. He was beginning to hate Shannon Shane…a lot.

"Uh, no, thank you. That won't be necessary."

"Very big, sir. Uh, *good.* Very good, sir." The little guy turned purple and fled.

Hal stood in front of the three-way mirror and wondered just what a "cool" guy did in *this* situation.

SIX PAIRS OF SHOES, three suits, two blazers. Six T-shirts made of silk woven by designer worms. Four pairs of casual slacks, two pairs of walking shorts and three pairs of jeans that Hal felt were too snug. "How am I supposed to get a wallet, cell phone and my dick in here all at the same time?" he asked. His concerns were addressed by an eye roll.

He didn't even want to know what he'd spent on the cashmere sweaters, the upscale ties, the multiple pairs of socks, the silver-handled umbrella, the leather satchel or the elaborate shoe-care kit. Oh, and the belts, silk boxers and *shoe trees*.

"You're not working under the illusion that I'll actually use those, are you?"

"Close your eyes and sign here, Hal. There's a good boy."

"Has anyone ever told you that you're patronizing and obnoxious?"

"I just love compliments. Now take the pen."

"Do I have any money left?"

"Money?" Shannon threw back her head and laughed. "Hal, honey. This is credit. But we're opening a series of store charges so that you can save ten to fifteen percent. That's a lot of money saved right there."

Hal dug his hands into his pockets. "How come I have to spend so much in order to save?"

"It's just the law of retail," Shannon told him, pulling his hands out of his pockets. "Don't do that. You look like an overgrown teenager."

"Aw, for chrissakes—"

"Shoulders back! Stomach in! Cock one hip. Good," said his drill sergeant. "Now, casually drape one arm along the counter. Excellent."

He curled his lip at her.

"Stop that. Turn to Lana," she instructed.

Lana was their current salesperson, engaged in packaging all of his new silk boxers. He looked at her, and she looked up at him, raising an eyebrow at Shannon.

"Now smile," said his tormentor. "Smile at Lana like she's the only woman in the world."

"Cheese," said Hal. "This is beyond cheesy…" But somewhere along the way, he did aim a genuine smile in her direction.

Lana blinked and a dreamy expression came over her face. She smiled back. Then she said, "Wow."

Wow? Did she mean this stuff actually worked? Hal kept his shoulders straight and then folded his arms on the counter and leaned in just a tad. He decided to experiment.

"Lana, I'm in training here. I haven't graduated yet from Suave School. But I have to say that you have the most beautiful eyes."

The woman, probably in her midforties, blushed and dimpled. "Oh, thank you. Aren't you sweet." She stuck some kind of gold sticker on the tissue paper she'd wrapped around the boxers. "You know, I think I can give you another special discount on these…let me see if I can find the code." She rummaged around. "Yes! Here it is."

And just like that, Hal learned the power of charm and image.

Shannon dug him in the ribs with her elbow as they walked out. "See? A smile, a little easy confidence and good grooming. They will get you everywhere. You gonna listen to me now?"

Hal all but staggered under the combined weight of the shopping bags. "Are we done yet?"

"One more stop at a sporting goods store. We need to get you outfitted for the gym."

He groaned. "You are relentless. Why does it matter what I wear when I sweat?"

"Are you kidding me?" Shannon stared at him. "This could be the most important part for your social life, Hal."

"Huh?"

She gazed at him with something akin to pity. "You're going to be picking up *chicks* in the gym."

"Chicks," repeated Hal.

"Yes," she told him. "So you've got to show all the right bulges in all the right places."

I got a bulge for you right here, baby. But he didn't say it aloud. He was pretty sure that sentiment crossed the line from "cool" to "disgustingly piggy."

So he just continued to drag their kill through the echoing, gleaming mall until they arrived at a he-man's paradise called Jock, Stock and Barrel. Leering in the window stood a shiny mannequin with Ricky Martin's face and Arnold Schwarzenegger's body. It had biceps like Popeye and wore microscopic, lime-green nylon shorts with a canary-yellow muscle T-shirt.

"No," said Hal, transfixed with horror. "I'm not setting foot in there." A man had to draw the line somewhere, didn't he?

12

"COME ON, HAL," SHANNON bullied him. "We're almost done." It had been a very long afternoon and she was tired. Spike-heeled boots might look killer, but they felt killer, too.

"Correction. We *are* done." And her client dug in his own heels. The formerly malleable Hal became a mule, and no matter what angle she took she could not find the carrot to move him forward.

She finally installed him back in her moldy beemer and put on some reggae music in the hopes that he'd unwind a little. She drove to a nearby strip mall and left him in the car with the packages while she went in and bought him some basic workout clothes in dark and neutral colors. She added white socks to the mix and then went and got him. "I can't just buy the cross-trainers and running shoes for you. You have to actually come in and test them for comfort."

She got him into this last store, stuck him on a vinyl bench and brought him several pairs of gym shoes. Then she drilled a rule into his head: *Thou Shalt Not Wear Running Shoes With Jeans.*

"Why not?" asked Hal.

"Just repeat after me. 'I, Hal Underwood, will not under any circumstances pair my running shoes with jeans or any other slacks.'"

"What about sweatpants? Shorts?"

She sighed. "How about, 'I, Hal Underwood, will *only* wear running shoes with sweatpants or shorts.'"

"I still don't understand why."

"Just promise!"

"What about cross-trainers?"

"Those are okay with jeans in extremely casual situations. But try to avoid that look. We're aiming for cool elegance."

"Suave School sucks, you know that? Gym shoes are comfortable. These lace-up things are not. If my little toes stay numb and eventually fall off, I'm suing you for replacements."

"Fine."

They at last agreed on one pair of trainers and one pair of running shoes. While the salesperson boxed them up and ran the total, Shannon patted Hal's shoulder. "This bill won't be so bad. You can even keep your eyes open. I'm just going to run out to the car for a sec, okay?"

He eyed her suspiciously.

"What?" she asked, all innocence.

Hal squinted.

She widened her eyes. Then she turned and walked out to the car. Keeping an eye on him through the large plate-glass window, she found the bag that contained his old clothes and shoes. She waited for him to look down and sign the credit card slip. Then, bag in hand, she sprinted for the Dumpster in the corner of the parking lot.

"I knew it!" he shouted, running after her. "You're evil!"

She picked up speed. The spike-heeled boots didn't help, but this was her only shot.

"Give me that bag!" Hal yelled, his footsteps getting closer and closer.

Crap! She was five feet from the Dumpster and closing. She looked over her shoulder. His blue eyes blazed at her, less than a yard away.

Shannon used her back heel as a springboard and leaped forward. He lunged at the same time and caught her by the back of the sweater and one silver leather belt loop.

She twisted, yanked and heard a disturbing rip— the sound of stitching giving way. Her pants! He was ruining her four-hundred-dollar designer pants!

Furious and more determined than ever, Shannon vaulted forward and up, slam-dunking the bag of clothes into the filthy Dumpster and hanging from it by the armpits.

A sickening smell assaulted her nose just as Hal grasped her around the hips. "You—you—you! I can't believe you just did that!"

There was a half-gnawed potato skin under her left arm, and her right hand had landed in what looked like the remains of a chicken sandwich, garnished with rotted lettuce. "I can't believe I did, either." But she saw with satisfaction that the bag containing his awful clothes had spilled during flight, and the contents lay scattered in a deep, stinky central crater.

She relaxed, intending to drop backward into Hal's arms. Mission accomplished!

Except…his hands weren't easing her down as she'd expected. No, they were— *Oh, God! Oh, no!*

Hal was boosting her upward. And forward. And—"Help! Nooo!"

"Gosh," he said. "I seem to remember yelling that word, too. But it didn't do any good."

"Nooo!" she yelled again, scrabbling among paper drink cups, oily wet wrappers, a bag of lawn clippings and a rusty hubcap. The potato skin and the chicken sandwich had only served to grease her way forward. Oh, dear God— Was that a…? *No,* if she touched that she would just die.

A scuffling sound toward the left corner of the Dumpster reminded her that she probably had rats in there for company. *"Heellpp!"* she shrieked. "I'm sorry, I'm sorry! Don't drop me in here, Hal, *please!*"

"I don't know a single reason why I shouldn't," he growled. "You so deserve it."

"I will be your *sex slave* for the next entire week if you'll just pull me out," promised Shannon.

He hesitated.

"The next month! Two months!"

Just as she almost lost her struggle to keep her face

out of a mound of barbecued chicken bones, Hal tugged on her ankles and pulled her, inch by inch, back over the rim of the Dumpster.

Her sweater was coated with sour cream and coffee grounds. She had potato peels in her hair. Her silver leather pants were streaked with ketchup, mustard, rust, grime and something utterly unspeakable. But Shannon had never felt so grateful.

"Thank you, thank you, thank you," she said, panting for breath.

"Are you okay?" he asked gruffly.

She nodded. But along with her breath, a natural urge for revenge returned. All she was guilty of was getting rid of some perfectly awful, dated clothing! She'd done the guy a service. And he'd pushed her into the garbage....

Shannon stood up and pushed the hair back from her face. She looked at Hal, who looked back at her with a combination of anger and sheepishness.

"My hero," she said soulfully. Then she hugged him.

SHANNON LAY neck-deep in scented bubble bath in her Avon apartment, surrounded by a fashion magazine, a lighted candle and a glass of wine.

She'd dropped her own clothes into a plastic garbage bag this time, and it sat near the door, ready to go to the cleaners. Though she'd tied the top of the bag into a knot, eau de Dumpster still wafted through the air.

She submerged herself and blew the scent, along

with some bubbles, out of her nostrils. When she came up, water streaming off her face and shoulders and freshly washed hair, the air seemed better.

She thought of Hal's outraged expression when she'd hugged him and laughed. He had announced she was fired and barely spoken to her on the ride home in the now doubly defiled beemer.

Shannon watched water drip off her breasts and back into the tub. She'd always wondered where she'd gotten these honkers. Rebecca Shane was flat as a board, and her father's mother hadn't had a lot in the chest, either. So who did Shannon have to thank for her boobs?

They'd been dangling over several hundred pounds of garbage this afternoon—her first ever Dumpster-diving experience. But what if her real father was a sanitation worker? And maybe her real mother cleaned houses or worked as a data-entry clerk or did sewing alterations for a living?

She had no idea. She had to track them down. While she didn't want to hurt her adoptive parents, they had lied to her by omission.

All she knew was a few sketchy details and the fact that she'd been fostered by the New England Home for Little Wanderers for a few short weeks. So at least her biological parents hadn't sold her on the black market. She supposed that was something to be thankful for.

Shannon added some more hot water to the tub and felt tears trying to form in the backs of her eyes. She blinked them away.

Hal's voice echoed in her head. *I'm here if you need to talk.*

"No, you're not," she said aloud. "You just fired me." She stuck a toe out of the water and peered at the chipped purple polish on it. She plunked it down into the bubbles again.

But did he really mean it? He'd probably just said it in the heat of the moment. He didn't want to fire her—he needed her too much. And…oh, no. Finesse needed her to keep this gig. It was her responsibility, same as Jane's, to keep their doors open.

She clenched a wet, soapy fist and brought it down on her knee. Great. She'd been impulsive and irresponsible again, gone and hugged him to smear him with garbage. She might have done it to get even, but they wouldn't have been near the Dumpster at all if she hadn't thrown his old clothes into it.

Shannon stood up and reached over to the bathroom countertop for her cordless phone. Then she settled back into the water and dialed Hal's number.

"Am I really fired?" she asked when he answered.

"I haven't decided yet."

She swallowed. "Oh."

"Is that the reason you called?"

Well, I kind of wanted to hear your voice. "Sort of."

"That doesn't tell me much, and I'm really annoyed at you," he said.

"Yeah. I know. But you don't want to fire me, really."

"Why not?"

"Because I promised to be your sex slave, remember?"

She heard a swift intake of breath, and then only dead silence on the other end of the line. "I don't have any clothes on right now," she said. "I'm in the bathtub with the lights turned low, wearing nothing but bubbles." She heard him exhale, but still he said not a word.

"Would you like to come join me?" she prompted.

"More than anything."

She smiled in satisfaction. He was a typical, predictable man. He wasn't going to fire her.

"But I'm not coming over."

Her smile faded. "Why not?"

"Because for one thing, I'm still pissed. And I have yet to hear an apology. Those clothes might have been rags to you, but did you ever stop to think that they might have had sentimental value for me?"

"No," she admitted. "I'm…I'm sorry. In my experience guys aren't too sentimental over stuff like that."

"Yeah. Let's *talk* about your experience with guys. Because that's another reason I'm not coming over. You complain that you get used for your looks, Shannon, and I've seen the hurt that causes you. But you're stuck in the same old cycle. You use your beauty, too. What did you do when you heard I might fire you? You played on your looks and offered me sex."

She swallowed and felt the prick of tears again.

"Well," Hal continued, "I'm not going to be like

the other guys you've known. The other guys who just want to screw you. I'm only human, and I have a hard time turning you down in person, but I'm not falling for it this time. I want to actually make love to you, not just have a quickie on a desk or in my kitchen. A *screw.*"

It was her turn not to say anything.

"I'm not firing you, Shannon. But that decision has nothing to do with your looks or with sex. I'm making my decision because even though you're arrogant and somewhat unstable—not to mention being a denim thief—you're damned good at what you do."

"I'm just a failed actress with an attitude, Hal."

"I disagree. I really will fire you if you don't stop talking to yourself like that. Got it?"

"Yeah." She reached for her glass of wine, making a small splash, and took a sip.

Hal's voice changed on the other end of the line. It thickened. "What did you say you were wearing again?"

"A few bubbles. Why?"

"Because…I'd like to make love to you right now, but without seeing you. I want to give you an orgasm over the phone."

13

SHANNON'S MOUTH went dry, and she licked her lips. "You do?"

"Oh, yeah. And I will."

"How?"

"First of all I want you to close your eyes and lie back in the tub," he said in husky tones.

She did.

"You have a sponge?"

"Yes."

"Take the sponge and let it absorb water. Let it float with you. Now, move your hand to your knee and stroke up your thighs. Touch your stomach, trail your fingers around you to your waist so that you're hugging yourself. Move them to your shoulder.

"Your breasts are heavy and they're squished inside your arms. It hurts just a little, doesn't it?"

"Yes," she whispered.

"But in a good way. Ease your hand off your shoulder and move it down to cup your breast, squeeze it like I want to, caress that smooth, tender skin."

Shannon did.

"Now rub your palms over the nipple, around and around, and imagine it's in my mouth. I'm sucking hard, pulling your desire from it and drinking it in. I'm flicking my tongue against it and loving it. Keep rubbing…mmm.

"Now the other nipple's in my mouth and I'm scraping it lightly with my teeth. I'm doing everything to it that I want to do to you between your legs. I am all tongue and wet heat and I want you spread out for me like a feast."

She couldn't help a moan as she pleasured her own breasts, her steps choreographed to the sexy vibrations of his voice. She could feel the tones of him in the very center of her, as if he were delicately strumming her clitoris, heating it like an hors d'oeuvre.

"Move your hand from your breasts down to your ribs and belly. Then slide it under you and over that hot, sweet ass of yours, Shannon. Caress that like I want to…imagine that's my hand there. Curl your fingers into forbidden places and stroke yourself where it's slick and plump and ready for me to eat."

She gasped as she touched herself, slid her fingers back and forth along the submerged folds, imagining his mouth there as he talked dirty to her.

"Now move your hand around to the front and touch your clit, but only once. Don't be greedy."

She whimpered, wanting to stay there and play a little. She touched herself again.

"Get your hands out of the cookie jar, naughty girl," Hal said into her ear, and she jumped.

"How did you know what I was doing?"

"I just did. Because I want to do it, too." He chuckled. "Now get the sponge and spread your thighs...arch your back and poke out of the water just barely. Feel the cold air? Squeeze water out of the sponge onto yourself."

Hal was breathing heavily into the phone now.

"Are you hard?" she whispered, once again submerged in the water.

"Yes!"

"Do you want me? To be inside me?"

"Yeah... Now, move. The. Sponge," Hal said in tight, strained, tones. "Back. And. Forth. Between. Your. Legs."

She did, and the soft sea-foam tickled and teased, awakened and tortured every sexual nerve she had. Water sluiced out of it, too, adding to the sensations.

Her breathing became rough, ragged.

"Are you touching yourself?" Hal asked. "Imagining it's me?"

"Yes..."

"My mouth, even?"

"Mmm-hmm. Yes," she agreed again, moving the sponge faster and raising her hips from the water again. Her foot knocked the stopper from the drain, but she didn't care.

All she cared about was Hal's voice, and the pleasure she was steeping in, and the tension that climbed higher and higher. She cared about the sponge and the swirling, eddying, just-out-of-reach climax that she knew was coming.

"Aaaahhhhh," he breathed into the phone.

She agreed with that, too.

He let go a string of heartfelt curses followed by a long groan, and the sounds he made turned her on so much that she slipped over the edge. She exploded with him in perfect harmony.

HAL HAD NEVER had phone sex until these past few minutes. He figured that for a computer geek with only semiexistent social skills, he'd done pretty well. Shannon's soft sighs were still audible through the receiver of his phone.

Part of him wished that she lay naked beside him, here in his bed. Another part of him was still aroused that she'd let her own fingers do the walking…with his guidance.

"This was a hell of a lot better than going to meet some personal trainer," he said.

"I called him and told him we weren't going to make it," she murmured drowsily.

"Well, we *did* make it. Just not with him."

"Ha-ha."

"Don't fall asleep in that tub," he warned.

"'Kay. It's getting cold in here anyway, half the water's gone and I'm turning all wrinkly."

He chuckled.

"Hey, Hal?"

"Hmm?"

"Thanks for not firing me. And if you promise not to wear them in public, I'll take you to the Goodwill store to see if we can locate your other old jeans."

"They're probably gone by now," he said, his tone pessimistic.

"Well, yeah," she agreed. "I'm counting on that. But I thought I'd make the offer."

He choked. "You are not a nice woman." He could practically hear the grin spreading over her face.

"I never claimed to be the kind of girl you could take home to Mama, Hal."

"Are you kidding? My mother would love you. She wears black leather pants, too. She's a poet. She even performs in public, God help us all."

"That's so cool!"

Hal snorted. "She speaks only in rhyme. Now, the iambic pentameter stuff I can deal with—it's the haiku that sends me right over the edge."

"Mom sounds fascinating. Where does she do her readings?" Shannon actually seemed interested.

"At a progressive nightclub down near the city and in an artsy café/bookstore in Hartford. She has a thing coming up that I'll have to go to. Wanna come?"

"It's a date," said Shannon. It sounded like she was drying off with a towel while she talked. The thought of her naked body aroused him all over again, but he sternly turned his thoughts elsewhere.

Shannon Shane was only marking time with him, and he needed to accept that. But he'd enjoy it while it lasted.

LATER, because he couldn't sleep, Hal drove to the office to continue his search for the information leak. Greer Conover had announced the development of a product series far too close to what Underwood Technologies was offering.

He'd tried to tell himself he was paranoid, but the timing of the man's announcement was just too suspect. While he wasn't a bad programmer, Greer was simply not innovative enough to have dreamed up a similar product. And with the IPO around the corner, Underwood Tech's stock would take a nosedive if Conover's package hit the market within a few months. They'd lose their competitive edge.

Hal had already spent countless hours looking for signs of outside hackers, but he'd turned up absolutely nothing suspicious. He was forced back to the conclusion that the information leak was internal to his own company.

He was now facing probably weeks of detective work, checking the exchange server. Rubbing at his eyes, he went to the machine in the lobby of the building and bought not one but two sodas, full sugar and full caffeine.

Time to hit the e-mail server and sort in descending order by size. He'd have to look at every single e-mail, to whom it was sent and what had been attached. If that didn't turn up anything, he'd have to sort in ascending order by addressee and see if the names of Conover or any of his staff turned up.

However, the guy would be stupid to be that blatant. Which meant that Hal was going to have to look at the Internet logs of various individual workers at Underwood Technologies. That was hit or miss and he'd go cross-eyed and then blind during the process.

He popped the top on one of the Cokes and inhaled half of it, while the worst possibility hit him. Anyone in the company with access to the server could have burned files onto a CD or a flash card or an external hard drive and simply walked the information out of the building.

The theft would be virtually undetectable.

Hal cracked his neck and wondered if he was going to have to install hidden security cameras in every corner. It went against the grain, not to mention the prohibitive expense involved.... ·

He sighed, went back upstairs and got to work. Things had been easier in a lot of respects when they'd been a three-man shop, not a company of forty-five employees.

He wished he could access even a smidgen of the code Greer was using. Because every programmer wrote code in a different way...and Hal would be able to tell if Conover had pirated work done by a programmer at Underwood Tech. He'd recognize the sequences just like handwriting.

He drained the rest of soda number one and popped open the second can. But if he hacked into Conover's info to check on the guy, he'd be descending to his level. And while Hal might need some sessions at Suave School, he was not a cockroach.

His thoughts turned to Shannon again as he entered commands into his computer. *Focus on the problem at hand, you dumb son of a bitch. Shannon Shane is in your life right now because you are paying her. You'd best remember that, even if you're getting some perks on the side.*

SHANNON PULLED on a pair of flannel pajamas and twisted her hair into its habitual knot. She made a bowl of microwave popcorn and flopped on her couch, where she fell asleep watching reruns of *Will & Grace.* Three hours later, she found herself sitting at a White House dinner. She was dressed in a ripped World Peace T-shirt and ratty jeans, and she'd acquired a tattoo of a sunflower on her left arm.

She looked up from her endive salad to find that she, a lone Democrat, sat at a table of fifty disapproving Republicans. They didn't like her toe ring, they didn't like her tattoo, and they wouldn't pass her the salt. At the head of the table sat the president.

"See what I mean?" he asked the rest of them. "I did the right thing by giving her up for adoption."

She awoke in a cold sweat and blinked. A bad movie unfolded on the television—something to do with a psychic mule. She shut off the set. Her popcorn still sat in front of her, along with the saltshaker that nobody in the dream would pass.

She grabbed for this, dumped a quarter of the container onto the popcorn and began to munch.

Horrid dream. She checked her arm, just in case, for the sunflower tattoo. Thank God it wasn't there.

But it was obvious she couldn't go on like this. She'd go nuts wondering about her biological parents if she didn't take some steps to find them. She supposed she should start with the adoption agency.

Shannon went to her laptop and logged on to the Internet. She found the Home for Little Wanderers site easily and discovered that she could, in fact, do a search.

She began to proceed and then froze. What if…what if she didn't like the results? What if she discovered things she didn't really want to know?

She logged off, feeling nauseated, and folded her hands on top of the laptop. Warm from the electrical current and batteries, it hummed under her palms, which began to sweat.

She could do one of two things at the moment. She could write a letter for the Home's files, which would give her biological mother or father an update on her life and/or even grant permission for them to contact her.

Or she could initiate a full-fledged search by the agency to locate her true parents. Either way, they would have to agree to any request by her to contact them. Their privacy had to be respected.

Shannon slowly ate another handful of popcorn. If her parents had been young college students at the time of her birth, then they very probably had other families by now. Each of them could have two, three or four other children—and spouses that they'd never told. She couldn't simply turn up one day and disrupt their lives.

What if neither parent wanted to meet her? Or perhaps only one did? What would she do? Would the sense of rejection grow even stronger and eat her alive?

On the other hand, there might be a letter from one or both of them in her file, just waiting for her to discover it and contact them.

The Home for Little Wanderers was located in Boston. Did her mother still live there? Her father? Did she have siblings?

Her mind took her back to Rebecca Shane, and how she'd imparted this earth-shaking information so calmly over a salad of field greens. Shannon began to shake. She should have dumped the salad over Rebecca's head.

But, no. Her mother hadn't been as calm as she'd liked to have been. Her hands had trembled as she lifted her wineglass, and deep, dark shadows had marred her lovely eyes. It hadn't been easy on Rebecca. And at least she'd forced herself to finally tell the truth. She'd faced her daughter, unlike Shannon's father.

Shannon reached the very bottom of the bowl of popcorn, which now contained only hard kernels. She put a couple into her mouth and crunched on them, staring once again at her computer.

Go on, do it. Start a search.

I don't know if I can handle the results. I just don't know.

Coward. How can you just not do anything?

I'm not a coward. The people who raised me are my parents. For better or worse. Whether or not we agree about fashion, politics or even religion. My mother is my mother…and I feel that searching for another one dishonors her, somehow.

That's a cop-out.

No, it's an opt-out. For the moment. After all, I'm the wild and unpredictable Shannon. Who knows how I'll feel tomorrow?

14

SUAVE SCHOOL started bright and early the next morning as Hal yawned his way into the gym. He spied Shannon easily by just following the gazes of every other man in the place. They were all trained on her body, while she, oblivious wearing a set of headphones, worked out like a madwoman on an elliptical machine.

Hal checked his watch and wondered how long she'd been at it. She was damp with sweat and her face shone pink under the lighting. Though the woman would still look edible if she'd been rolled through tar, her eyes looked puffy, as if she hadn't slept.

That made two of them. Hal folded his arms and gazed at all the other men checking out Shannon. An older guy with a pinky ring and a gold chain around his neck couldn't take his eyes off her breasts. An overtanned creep who looked like a refugee from *Baywatch* was absorbed in her rear end. A stocky college kid with a buzz cut appeared dazzled by the entire package. And yet another man lost his footing on a stair-climber and almost fell off while checking out her legs.

None of them had given her an orgasm over the phone. He allowed himself a small, private grin and made his way over to her, trying to straighten his posture and suck in his stomach as she'd instructed.

Hey…hey, behold the stud! He caught sight of himself in the athletic club's wall of mirrors. While his skin was still fish-belly white, he didn't look half bad. He even got a couple of glances from women as he crossed the room.

Shannon saw him, waved and then frowned.

What? Did he have a coffee stain on his shirt? Hal looked down. Nope.

"Cool," she said as he approached, "does not mean walking like a rapper."

"Huh?"

She pulled off her headphones but didn't slow down. "You're doing something screwy with your head and you're bouncing in the knees when you walk."

"Well, good morning to you, too. All I'm doing," Hal retorted, "is keeping my shoulders back and sucking in my stomach, like you said."

"Well, that part is good. Just leave your knees out of it and don't swing your arms. And don't do that thing with your neck—you look like a bobble-head."

"Bobble-head," Hal repeated, with growing wrath. "You didn't seem to think I was a bobble-head *last night.*" His chest swelled and he looked down at her from his superior height.

"Perfect," said Shannon. "Oh, very good! It's that kind of…casual arrogance…that we're looking for. But no grimacing. It's got to be a *friendly* casual arrogance."

Hal stared at her. "You are the devil."

"No. But you can think of me as an overgrown satanic elf, if you'd like. Now, hop onto this thing," she commanded, getting off the elliptical machine. "We'll start you out with some cardio." In the absence of the personal trainer, she was in charge.

Thirty minutes later she'd worked him into a soggy pulp. "Have you ever," he gasped, "heard of starting at the beginning? With reasonable, manageable goals?"

"No time for that crap," Shannon said cheerfully. "We gotta make a he-man out of you in just a couple of weeks." So saying, she slapped him on the ass.

Hal froze.

"C'mon," she called, walking toward the weight room.

He sprang at her, furious, and caught up. He snaked an arm around her shoulders and honked a hooter.

Outraged, she turned on him. "What in the *hell* do you think you're—"

"Do not. Ever. Slap my ass. In public. Again."

She opened and closed her mouth.

"Understood?" Every man in the entire gym stared at them, expecting her to level him.

"Message received, loud and clear," she said. And then she added, "Sorry."

Hal relented. "But you can slap my ass in private, if you want."

"I'll keep that in mind."

"I might even demand it, since after all, you're my sex slave for the next couple of months." He grinned. "Remember?"

She snapped her fingers in mock sorrow. "Damn. And I left my rubber dress and cat-o'-nine-tails in L.A."

Hal lifted a brow, intrigued. "We could always order a replacement dress, you know."

"Is that right." She directed him to the lateral pull-down machine and started stacking it with weights. "Sit."

"I thought the master gave the orders."

"Not in the gym. Now let's get to work."

HAL LAY in a tanning booth in Betsy's 'Burban Beach and tried to ignore the annoying buzz of the thing. His eyes were covered with weird little goggles and he had placed nasty whitening strips on his teeth which oozed evil gel. They thoroughly disgusted him and made his chompers sensitive to hot and cold.

He ached all over from Shannon's workout, which had tortured muscles he hadn't even known he'd had.

In short, this whole process of becoming a stud was totally emasculating, and the irony of that was not lost on him. He felt like a lab rat.

Worse, he was a lab rat wearing a tube sock and nothing else.

He wasn't stupid: he'd heard all sorts of horror stories about people who got sensitive parts of them fried in tanning beds.

In fact, he could swear that his buns were smoking right now. And he was going to have to come up with a good story for people at work. How would he explain his metamorphosis from glow-in-the-dark pale to savagely tan?

The more he thought about it, the more ridiculous this seemed. Even Hal had heard of bronzing cream. Couldn't Shannon just smear some of that crap on his face?

Hal shifted, adjusted the tube sock and began to sweat. He did not feel like a stud. Even Mr. Universe couldn't feel like a stud under these circumstances. He'd had it.

He pushed up the lid of the lighted coffin and sat up. The stupid little goggles fell to the floor. He let the tube sock drop to the floor, too, and pulled the disgusting whitening strips out of his mouth. He tossed them into the trash.

Then he spoke directly to man's best friend and life partner. "I'm glad you're not toasted, there, buddy. Sorry I had to sock it to you…yeah, I know that was bad."

He stood up and shut the lid of the human roaster. He stuffed himself into his new clothes and took a swipe at his hair, which now fell in an ingenious wind-blown mess without him doing anything to it at all.

And then he marched out to the reception area and the teenage Paris Hilton lookalike who'd sold him the tanning package. "I want a refund," said Hal. "I am not doing this."

In a few minutes he opened the door to the cool April air and smelled freedom from feminine tyranny! One step. Two steps. He was almost outside when the Paris clone called, "Sir?"

Hal turned, raising an eyebrow.

"Sir, do you want your…tube sock?" She was holding it by a thread and trying to keep a straight face.

It was a perfectly good sock. One that Shannon hadn't swiped and thrown away. He saw no reason to waste it. "Thank you," Hal said with great dignity. He took it and left.

"WE ARE NOW in stage two of training," said Shannon, circling Hal and evaluating every inch of him. She had invaded his office.

"Uh-huh," said Hal, who was hunched over his computer.

"Stage two means further development of stage one, but new work to do on posture—" she poked him in the spine "—conversation/social skills and media training."

Hal ignored the poke and kept searching employee Internet logs.

Shannon poked him again.

"Didn't I fire you?" he muttered.

"You thought better of it. Now, straighten up, Mr. Underwood." She moved to the other side of his desk and sat in the visitor's chair.

"Were you schooled by the Gestapo?"

"Quit whining."

To her satisfaction, Hal gave up and pushed back from his computer. "You're early. By my watch, I still had seven minutes of freedom."

She grinned sadistically at him. "I just couldn't *wait* to see you."

"Mmm. Well, here's what I'm thinking. As my sex slave, you should now get down on your knees and bark like a dog." Hal shot her an evil grin.

She narrowed her eyes at him. "And here's what I'm thinking. *Not a chance in hell.*"

"Insubordination from the slave leads to all kinds of dire consequences," Hal murmured thoughtfully. A wolfish expression spread across his face.

"I could quit, you know."

He rubbed at his chin. "It'd save me from having to fire you again. But you'd have to remain my sex slave. You gave me your word that if I pulled you out of the Dumpster, I could have my way with you for two months."

She raised her chin. "I was…under duress."

"Oh, here come the excuses."

"I could probably even sue you for sexual harassment."

"Oh, yeah? Who brought up the whole sex slave thing to begin with? And how many witnesses saw *you* slap *my* ass at the gym? I think you'd better think that one over before you act on it." Hal lounged back in his chair.

"I was kidding. I wouldn't sue you."

"Oh? Why not?"

Shannon found herself admiring the rangy lines of his body and the raw intelligence of his face. His eyes held a mocking twinkle to which she couldn't help but respond. "Because…I like you, Underwood."

"You like to bully me."

"No. Well, yes." She grinned. "But I do really like you. You're a good guy."

Hal leaned forward. "Oh, yeah? So what am I good at?"

Her cheeks warmed. She gestured toward Hal's server room and the whole floor. "Technology and programming, obviously."

He stood up and moved around the desk, his hands shoved into his pockets as usual. "And?"

Her heartbeat quickened. "And…business. You're about to go public, after all." She tugged on his wrists. "Get your hands out of your pockets."

"What else am I good at, Shannon? Hmm?" He leaned over her and shot her a bona fide stud grin.

Wow, he sure learns fast….

He allowed her to pull his hands out of his pockets, but he caught one of hers. A flash of heat went through her body as he guided *her* hand toward his pocket, inserted it, and moved it inward toward the hard ridge that had appeared under his fly.

Her breath caught.

He put his thumb in the center of her bottom lip and rubbed it gently back and forth, looking down at her with an enigmatic expression. She caught it in her teeth and bit it lightly. Smoothed her tongue over the tiny ridges and whorls in the skin. Watched him catch his own lower lip between his teeth, and his pupils dilate.

Hal took his thumb back and then brushed his knuckles across one of her nipples. It was as if he'd pushed her On button—fire shot from the sensitive tip to her belly and between her legs.

She moved her head closer to his groin, her breath hot and teasing at his denim-covered erection. It swelled, straining to meet her lips.

Shannon removed her hand from his pocket and grabbed his hips, pulling them toward her. She placed her mouth directly over the top of his zipper and used her teeth to tug it down…one inch, then another and another.

She used her tongue to edge the fabric of his boxers back until she found just a tiny bit of flesh.

His breathing went ragged as she slowly licked it. She pulled her mouth away, looked up and smiled with the power of it—even though she knew what would happen next.

Just like any other man, Hal would grab the back of her head and pull forward, trying to grind her mouth against his penis.

He groaned, his eyes closed, and defied all her expectations. Hal simply ran a tender finger along her jaw. He caressed her lips again. He smoothed her hair.

She blinked with the shock of it. And then she said "thank you" in the only way she knew how. She placed her mouth on him again and eased more fabric aside. She kissed his exposed flesh. Moved her hands up to undo the button over his zipper. And took him, heavy and thick and muscular, out of his pants.

Hal gave an intense groan and groped behind him for the edge of his desk as she took just the tip into her mouth. She moved with him. She didn't particularly care for this, but she wanted to bring him pleasure.

He didn't try to ram himself into her mouth. He simply waited to see what she would do and expressed his appreciation for the gift.

She took her mouth away and caressed the shaft of him. How far was she willing to go?

Shannon bent her head as someone pounded on the door.

They both froze.

"Hey, Halibut! I got a—"

"No," thundered Hal. "Open that door, Ryan, and you are a *dead man.*"

15

Now what did they do? Hal quickly shoved his pal back into his pants and zipped up, though it was difficult under the circumstances.

Shannon, far from being shocked or mortified, just sat in his visitor's chair and laughed.

But even though they were decent at this point, how did he explain the urgency with which he'd forbidden Ryan to open the door?

"Do you want to get under the desk?" he asked Shannon.

"No. That just makes it look worse."

"True."

"Hal," called Ryan's voice. "I don't want to know what you're doing in there, but maybe the lack of a girlfriend is getting to you, bud."

"Cabela, this is not what you think. Now go away!"

His blond torturess was holding her sides.

"I can't believe he thinks I'm whacking off in my office!" Hal hissed at her.

"Well, it does look bad…"

"You might want to stop laughing for a minute and

realize that I'm trying to be a gentleman and save your reputation at the expense of my own, you ingrate!"

This set off another wave of laughter. "My *reputation?* What is this, *Gone with the Wind?*"

He stared at her, outraged, while she twisted her hair into a knot and secured it with an Underwood Technologies pen from his desk.

"Hal, honey. It's past the millennium and frankly, like Rhett, I don't give a damn." She headed toward the door and then cast a regretful glance over her shoulder at his still-raging erection. "Good luck with that."

She twisted the knob, pulled and Ryan fell into the room. Shannon prodded him with her toe. "What have we here?"

"That would be a specimen of Attorneyus Nosyus, a subset of the Lowlifeus variety," Hal said in scathing tones, fixing his counsel with a hard stare.

Ryan grinned weakly. Then, still on his knees, he gazed up at Shannon, slack-jawed. "Hot damn," he said. "What…so what do you charge?"

"Goddamn it, Cabela! She's not a—"

"*Much* more than you can afford," Shannon told him, and made her exit.

"THEN WHAT IN THE HELL is she doing with *you?*" Ryan had asked, before fleeing from Hal's office.

It was a really good question. Hal dug his fists into his tired eyes and thought about it. The goddess had gone down on her knees in front of him. She'd unzipped him, taken his penis out and—

Boing! It awoke with a vengeance.

"Stop that," Hal growled at the offending member. He grabbed two heavy software manuals off the bookshelf behind his desk and dropped them into his lap.

Now, where was he? Oh, yes. Shannon had been prepared to do something for him that probably wouldn't have given *her* much pleasure. *Why?*

He could understand the benefits to her of comfort sex or even just scratching an itch. But to put it crudely, goddesses didn't need to give head. By virtue of their looks alone, they were pretty much exempt from it, like a charity was exempt from federal taxes.

He was more than a little mystified. Hal picked up another company pen and spun it between his fingers, remembering how she'd shoved the other pen into that wild, untamable, sexy hair of hers.

Maybe she likes it.

Oh, get real. His sister Peggy's voice popped into his brain. They'd once had a discussion about men, women and sex. Peg had told him a few home truths. "No woman likes it. How would you like having something the size of a cucumber shoved down your throat?"

Hal winced. When he'd asked about those sexy moans a past girlfriend had made, and her assurances that she didn't mind, Peggy had snorted. She shot him a pitying glance. "God, you men really do live in fantasyland, don't you?"

So why…why had Shannon done it? Or started to?

Well, duh. The whole thing had just been designed as a tease, that's all. She would have gotten him all hot and bothered and then not followed through.

Hal forced himself to turn back to the Internet logs. Information leak? He had a leak in his brain. His gray matter was running out of the shell like raw egg white while he obsessed about sex with his image consultant. He couldn't operate a successful business like this. It was time to get back to work.

Ryan's sneakiness bothered him. There was a time when he'd have chalked it up to a boyish prank: a desire by Cabela to bust his balls later.

But under the circumstances, it raised the hairs on the back of Hal's neck.

"Hey, handsome…" Tina, his receptionist, poked her head in, her hand full of message slips.

Hal almost looked over his shoulder before he realized that she was talking to *him*. "Hi, Tina. Ha-ha."

"No joke! You are looking amazing these days. By the way, you forgot to pick up your messages when you came in." She undulated into his office in one of her small skirts and handed him the stack. Hal noticed that her bare legs were very tanned. Had she been to an electric beach, too?

"You can just put people through to my voice mail," he told her. "Really. You don't have to take messages."

"Oh, I don't mind." She smiled.

He opened his mouth to tell her that it wasn't a question of whether she minded—it was all about the most efficient use of her time—but he decided he'd just sound like a jerk. "How's the layout for the annual report going?"

"Good, good. Well, back to work with me!" Tina turned and left his office, wiggling in all the right places. He was human; he noticed. But the white streak on the back of her calf told him that she hadn't been to an electric beach: she was using a self-tanning product.

The world was a strange place: white people trying to turn themselves dark. Dark-skinned people trying to lighten theirs. It was all very silly. He thought of Shannon's Dr. Seuss wall calendar and the star-bellied sneeches.

The sneeches hopped in and out of a machine that put stars on their bellies when stars were in fashion, and removed them again when they were not. Shannon was trying to turn him into a star-bellied sneech. He preferred to be a sneech without.

"You're losing your mind, Underwood," he muttered to himself. And his affliction was directly traceable to Shannon Shane.

"I'M A REPORTER," Shannon said to Hal the next day.

"No, you're the devil."

They sat in the conference room of Underwood Technologies after chasing out Ryan and some members of his legal staff. Cabela, the little worm, had tried to mumble an apology to her. She'd raised a brow and patted him on the shoulder. "Wishful thinking," she'd said. "I understand."

It had been a masterful act of degradation, if she did say so herself. She was good in the role of bitch-goddess…if only she didn't feel so insecure and screwed up inside. She'd spent the night tossing and turning while various strangers jumped out of crowds in her dreams and claimed to be her parents. Gomer Pyle had announced he was her father, while Morticia Addams declared she'd breast-fed Shannon as a baby.

Now she sighed and tapped her legal pad with a number two pencil. "I am not the devil. We've had this conversation. Now, once again—I'm a reporter. Let's say I'm doing a feature on you and your company for the local TV station, okay?"

"Yup. I tell you that I have no time to talk with you and you can find out all you need to know on the Internet." He seemed to have said it just to annoy her.

"No." She stabbed toward him with the pencil. "First, you are all about my comfort, if the reporter is at your office. Would I like a seat? Would I like something to drink? How can you accommodate me?"

"Seems a little obsequious," Hal said.

"It's *polite*. And that's another thing. For a general television audience, you want to avoid five-dollar words like 'obsequious.' Nobody will know what it means. Say 'brownnosing' instead." She rubbed at her temple and then shook her head. "Actually, just say as little as possible, but be friendly and open."

"You'd pay five bucks? Just for 'obseq—'"

"Hal! Stop being a smart-ass. We have a limited amount of time here. And—" she frowned at him "—why aren't you starting to show some color?"

"Uh—"

"You're not going to the tanning place, are you?"

He shook his head.

"Damn it, Hal! We don't have much time! Your first interview is when? Next Thursday? That is less than a week away."

"I want to use a bronzer instead," he told her. "If it's absolutely necessary. I hate lying in that coffin thing, and the little tartlet in charge made fun of my sock."

She knit her brow. "Your sock?"

"The tube sock."

Shannon put a hand over her mouth and stared at him. "You didn't really…oh, Hal! I was kidding about that!"

"A guy can never be too careful."

She laughed until her ribs hurt. Hal really was borderline hopeless, even if he was starting to become very good-looking. Finally, when she caught her breath, she said, "Show me your teeth."

"I'm not using those whitening strips, either. Those things ooze gooey gel, they're disgusting and they make me drool. I hate them."

"I make you drool, too, but you don't hate me, right?"

"You want the truth or a nice lie?"

"Ouch. Well, since I'm teaching you how to churn

out those nice lies, then lay one on me, baby." She braced herself.

He stared at her, his blue eyes intense under the knit eyebrows. His arms were folded across his chest.

"Body language is important, Hal," she said. "Your position right now is defensive, guarded and—"

"I only hate you about twenty hours out of the twenty-four," he said in a considering tone. "I don't hate you at all when we're acting on our, uh, animal magnetism. I do hate you when—"

"—hostile."

"—you poke me, prod me, lecture me and in general look me in the teeth."

"But that's my job!" she almost wailed. Then she recovered. "And you're supposed to be telling me nice lies! What you're telling me is the naked, ugly truth."

He seemed to take pity on her. "I don't really hate you twenty hours out of the day. Probably only about eight or nine. Is that more acceptable?"

"Definitely." She went back to being flip again. But she didn't want Hal to hate her at all. She wanted him to like her…a lot. "I can handle being hated during business hours. And let me remind you that you are paying me to look you in the teeth. Remember?"

"Yeah. That is a bummer. And very warped, too, paying thousands of dollars for a beautiful woman to insult me, manhandle me, steal my clothes, flog me into exercising and try to dye various parts of my body."

"I'm not that bad…"

"You are very, very bad," Hal said softly. His eyes

darkened and gleamed. "You are my dream bad girl." He slapped his hands on the table. "It's dangerous, in fact, for me to be around large flat surfaces when you're near. I want to pull you onto them, naked, and take you for a spin."

"Do you ever think about anything besides sex?"

"Yes. But it's regrettable."

"Do you ever think about *me* in any other context?"

He nodded. "A lot."

"I mean as more than a taskmaster and a tormentor."

He grinned. "I know what you meant. And the answer is, again, yes. I still wonder what it was that had you so upset the day we met. I wonder whether you sleep on your stomach or side or back. I debate whether or not you wear funny socks under those CFM boots of yours."

Her insides started to melt into a marshmallowy goo. *Stop that! Where's your starch? Where's your Greenwich grit?*

But Hal continued, making it difficult for her to breathe. "I want to know what toothpaste you use, and whether or not you like Rocky Road ice cream… and when the hell you're going to take your car in to be cleaned and sterilized by a professional. I think about that day I first saw you—a wild, wet woman in leather driving in the rain with the top of her convertible down. At the time, I thought you were just crazy. Now, I think it had something to do with your upsetting news. Did it?"

She picked at her cuticles, then nodded.

"You're helping me out, Shan. Why don't we see if I can help you?"

She straightened her spine and rubbed at her neck. "This isn't something you can help with."

"I'll bet you're wrong," said Hal. "Why don't you try me?"

16

SHANNON LOOKED into those blue eyes of his and searched for her recklessness. She delved deep for the characteristics that allowed her to throw back her head and laugh at Cabela's assumption that she was a hooker. Where had her impulsiveness gone hiding? What had she done with her brazen side? When had her moxie evaporated?

Why did revealing a simple fact to this man seem dangerous?

It's not the fact itself. It's what he'll do with it. How much he'll see behind it.

Hal pushed back from the table and stood up, obviously disappointed in her. "My apologies," he said. "I forgot that you're all about image. We should stay on the surface and avoid any topic of depth."

"Don't sneer at me, Hal." She said it quietly, with a pleading note that she despised.

"You can take off your clothes for me, but you can't share something that upsets you. Explain that, why don't you? I really want to understand. Because I know you're not just a garden-variety slut."

Anger ignited deep within her. "No, I'm a hot-house slut, honey. Rare and expensive and complicated to take care of. So you keep that in mind before you go reaching for any more nectar." She stared him down until he finally looked away.

"I shouldn't have— I didn't mean—" Hal threw up his hands.

"Don't apologize now, Hal. You threw it out there. I did sleep with you after knowing you only six hours. Or somebody with the name Shannon Shane slept with you." She started to collect her things: legal pad, pen, take-out coffee cup.

"What the hell does that mean? And where do you think you're going?"

She finally dredged up a scrap, a torn edge, of recklessness and threw the information out there. "It means that the day before I met you I found out that I'm adopted! And touching you, sleeping with you, was a reminder that I was alive and could feel sensation, even though I was numb. I needed to know that even though my whole identity had just been ripped away, there was still somebody *there,* somebody for you to get inside."

She found her bag and tossed the pad and pen into it, then hitched the handles over her shoulder. "You want to call me a slut for that, you go right ahead. But you participated, too, buddy! And that means you wear the same label, because I'm not allowing any double standards."

She headed for the door.

"Where are you going?" Hal repeated, starting after her.

"Around the goddamned bend."

He caught her arm. "I didn't call you any names, okay? I said I knew you *weren't* a slut. You heard an accusation instead. I'm not judging you, Shannon. I'm just trying to understand you."

"Good luck," she muttered. "I don't understand myself."

"Do any of us understand ourselves? Really and truly?" His eyes reflected compassion. They were the blue of logic, but also the blue of soul. The blue of stability. And the blue of hope.

He smiled at her, and she realized she'd been staring for some time. "What do you see in there, Shan? In my eyes?"

She blinked, hesitated. "I don't have a name for it…other than…you. I just see you."

He nodded and cupped her chin. "And who am I?"

The warmth of his hand, the simple affection, the way he looked at her—all of it undid her. *"You,"* she repeated. "You're just you."

"Exactly." He said the word as if complimenting her for the most brilliant deduction ever made. Clearly the man was mad. A mad genius.

"Hal, are you feeling okay?"

"I'm fine," he said, tugging her over to the polished boardroom table. He pushed her in the small of the back so she bent over it.

"Hal, *no.* I am not getting naked with you on this particular flat surface!"

"Shh. Just look."

She saw her reflection mirrored in the glossy finish. "Yeah, so? What are we doing, playing Narcissus?"

"What do you see, Shannon?"

"Me," she said impatiently. "Now, can I—"

"Aha! You see *you.*"

Nuts. The man is stark-raving nuts.

He gazed at her expectantly.

"Yes? I. See. Me." She used the tolerant tone one might employ with a toddler.

"Then it doesn't matter who your biological parents are," Hal said triumphantly. "You are yourself, no matter what."

She chewed on his statement for a minute, then shook her head. "That's very New Age, but it's a meaningless truism. And it's way too simplistic for the way I feel."

He sighed. "I don't know dick about New Age. But if something is true, then it's not meaningless. And the way you feel is, in actuality, very simple."

"How do you know that?" Shan was starting to get annoyed.

"You feel that your identity is gone. Right?"

"In a nutshell."

"Well, it's not. Whether your father's name is Joe or Bob, you're still you. Whether your mother's name is Twinkie or Sue, you're still you. It doesn't change anything."

"Bullshit!" Shannon exclaimed. "Different parents would make me look different, change my characteristics, even my personality. My age. My health."

"Yes, they would. But you *don't* have any other parents."

"Yes, I do," she said with heavy patience. "The point is that I've just discovered them."

"You still have the same parents you've always had. The ones who conceived you, whether you knew about them or not."

"But—"

"You are still you."

"Yes, but—I am so confused! The issue here is that I was deceived, all my life, until now."

"I thought you said the issue was your identity," Hal reminded her.

Furious, she stamped her foot. "It *is!*"

He shook his head. "Nope. For the last time, let me point out that *you are still you.*"

She let out a primal scream. "But I could have turned out differently, don't you see?"

"You could have. But you didn't. So you know who you are. Clearly. Therefore, you have no identity crisis."

Shannon said something very rude to him.

"I'm just being logical," he said, the picture of calm.

"Stuff your logic! It doesn't make sense!"

"It's inherent in logic to make sense."

She wanted to hit him.

"Look, if you *want* to have an identity crisis, then

you go ahead and have one," Hal said, in long-suffering, indulgent tones. "I'm just telling you that there's no basis for it. You're being a drama queen."

Her mouth dropped open. *Drama queen?* How could he say such a thing to her, given the circumstances? Shannon itched to beat on him, strangle him, Bobbit him. She struggled mightily with her urge for violence. At last she shrieked, "I hate men!" She whacked him in the chest with her bag and flew for the door.

"This is why I don't like to tell guys anything," she yelled, wrenching it open.

"What?" Hal stood mystified. "I solved your problem!"

"You did *not* solve it. You negated it. And then you insulted me, too! I am *not* a drama queen. And if I want my identity crisis, then I'll goddamned well have it!"

"I told you to go ahead!"

"I don't need your permission," she screamed.

"I give up," said Hal, as she slammed the door.

"IT'S PENIS LOGIC," was Jane's evaluation. Shannon had spilled her annoyance to her friends over cosmopolitans later. They sat in the bar at Bricco, a cozy little restaurant in nearby West Hartford. Outside there were patches of a late spring snow on the ground, and lots of people heading home after work.

Lilia almost spit out her drink at the word *penis,* but recovered with her characteristic grace. Nobody passing by the big plate-glass window behind them would have noticed a thing.

"Yes, penis logic!" Shannon agreed. "What is *up* with that? Uh, no pun intended."

Lil choked again, but Jane laughed. "You shared a problem with him. He's a man. He felt that he had to solve it for you."

"But I didn't ask him to solve it! All I wanted to do was talk about it. He pressured me to talk about it. Then he tells me there's no problem, because my issue isn't logical!"

"Are you sleeping with Hal Underwood?"

Ugh. Okay, she'd dug around and found some leftover recklessness for Hal. Now she needed to find the dregs of some brazenness for Jane. She drew on her years of acting classes and produced a casually dismissive expression. "He's a client, Jane. I've only known him a week."

"I didn't ask you how long you'd known him." Jane pulled the slice of lime off her cosmo glass and squeezed more of its tart juice into the drink. "What I'm asking you is whether or not that was his butt-print on our reception desk."

Lilia's eyes widened to the size of dinner plates.

"I disinfected the entire thing," Shannon announced. "The butt-print is gone."

"You didn't?" asked Lil.

"She did," said Jane.

"*Eeeeeuuuuuwww.* That's a little skanky, don't you think?" Lilia pursed her lips.

"I am not skanky. Jane and Dominic have boinked in the office. You don't look at them like that! Besides, Lil, you should try it sometime."

Poor Lilia had blushed to the roots of her hair. She was the same color as her cosmopolitan. "How do you know I haven't…had relations…on a desk?" she asked, raising her little chin.

Shannon exchanged a glance with Jane and they both died laughing. Jane finally caught her breath and said, "Because I'm sure it's a social faux pas, and your granny panties would catch on the antique hardware."

Lil couldn't help but laugh, too, even though she looked perturbed. "Just because I won't wear thongs does not mean I wear grannies!"

"I'll bet they're down to your knees," teased Jane.

"No! You know about the panty hose thing."

That's right, Shannon remembered, she wore the control tops instead of panties for a smooth line under her clothes. "Lil, nobody wears panty hose anymore. Except for you."

"That's not true. And I am not continuing this discussion, not even with my two best friends. It's not proper."

"Can we discuss sex, politics and religion, then? All at once? Just to make you crazy?" Shannon winked at her.

"No."

"Wanna wear a pair of my leather pants?"

"Definitely not. Would you like me to hem them eight inches in order to wear them?"

"Definitely not."

"We agree, then," Lil told her, with a serene smile.

"Back to my original question," Jane said, without subtlety. "Are you seeing Underwood's wood?"

"Would that I were." Shannon grinned and tried to avoid the topic yet again. But Jane was like a rottweiler.

"How much wood would an Underwood sport, if an Underwood could sport wood?" she quipped.

"He can. And a lot. Can we leave it at that?"

"If you insist. It's not much fun, though."

"Pardon me if I don't want my love life to be a source of entertainment for you, Jane."

"Well, I enjoy it, too," admitted Lil. She turned pink again when Shannon glared at her. "Don't shoot me! Your love life *is* a soap opera. I like to live vicariously."

"*Was* a soap opera. And not really—I always ditch the guy before things get truly soapy. It might surprise you to know that I've been celibate for a year until recently."

"Wait a minute…" Lil's brow wrinkled. "Isn't Hal Underwood that guy who looks like a serial killer? The hairy one? I met him."

Jane smirked.

"Again, past tense. He *was* hairy. He is now clean-shaven and bears a striking resemblance to Viggo Mortensen. His eyes are spectacular." Shannon looked longingly at a pack of Marlboro Lights lying on the bar and felt the old familiar craving for nicotine, even though it had been six years since she'd quit.

She picked up her drink instead. There was something about a cosmopolitan that suited her: the color made it all-girl, but the martini glass added sophistication while the vodka gave it bite. The lime was an accessory, like a great necklace or the perfect pair of stilettos.

Jane's personality was more red wine or beer, but she didn't look completely out of place with liquor.

Lilia just wasn't a hard-alcohol girl. She looked most comfortable with a cup of hot tea, of course. But if Shan had to assign her a drink it would have to be sherry, in a tiny cut-crystal glass. On a wild night, perhaps white wine. Two cosmopolitans rendered Lil completely unable to drive, which was why she'd been nursing hers for a good hour.

"Back to penis logic," Jane said. "I think it's sweet that he wanted to help you solve your problem, even if he went about it in a very male way. He can't really help being a man."

"True," Shannon admitted.

"So are you going to track down your birth parents?" Lil asked.

"I don't know. I'm afraid to hurt my…my adoptive parents by doing that, even though I'm angry with them. I'm also afraid of what I'll find out. And my biological parents may not want to hear from me. It's possible that they just closed that chapter of their lives and moved on."

Jane put her hand on Shannon's arm. "But they might be thrilled to hear from you. They may have wondered all of their lives what happened to you and how you turned out. What you're like as a person."

Lil nodded. "There could be a letter in your file right now from one of them, just waiting to be discovered by you."

Shan took a large swallow of her drink and a deep breath. "Yes." She pressed her fingertips together, hard, to try to release some of the tension in her body. "I'm not ready to contact anyone," she said slowly. "But I am going to see if there's any communication from one or both of them in my file."

"That's a good, concrete step," Jane told her, and Lil nodded. "It will help you to make the next one, too."

The bartender cast a glance in their direction, to see if they needed another round. Shannon hesitated, torn by the desire to just let a fog of alcohol close her mind down. She shook her head and signaled for the tab. Neither Jane nor Lil would have another drink, and she herself didn't need one.

Much better to go to the gym early in the morning and work out her frustrations on a stair-climber or in the pool. Then she'd clear the air with Hal and put him through his paces. She planned to sweat the stupid male logic right out of him.

She also shouldn't be sleeping with the guy. Not only was he a client, but also she was too screwed up to be sleeping with *anyone* right now. Wasn't she?

17

SHANNON PACED her apartment later that night, her stomach growling. She hadn't wanted food earlier, when they were at Bricco, but now that she was hungry she had nothing to eat. She checked the refrigerator just to make sure, but it yielded nothing more than a half-full bottle of white wine, some ancient, dried-out rice and a withered lemon.

She pitched the container of rice and checked the cabinets. Hmm. Unless she wanted to eat stale fortune cookies smeared with mint jelly, she was out of luck.

Finally, she turned to the freezer, where she found ice-burned veggies, a bottle of vodka and a lonely, mangled fish stick. She pulled it out and dangled it between thumb and forefinger. It had obviously fallen out of the box she'd once had in there, and onto hard times.

She felt a lot like it looked. She was walking with it to the trash when the phone rang.

"'Lo," she said, sandwiching the receiver between her ear and shoulder in order to wash her hands.

"Hi, Shannon, it's Hal."

"My pal Hal! What's up?"

"I obviously upset you earlier and though I'm still not sure why, I wanted to apologize. Can we talk? I could come there, if you'd like."

She hesitated. Her apartment was a mess, and she had nothing to offer him besides vodka, straight up. But they did need to talk. "Okay. And I shouldn't have yelled at you, when you were trying to be nice. I'm sorry. Have you eaten?"

"Why, are you cooking?"

She laughed. "Hell, no. Unless you want a lone frozen fish stick on a bed of used coffee grounds and a fortune cookie for dessert."

"I think I'll pass, thanks. Would you like to go out?"

She'd been thinking more along the lines of take-out, but she said, "Sure." She gave him her address and made a reservation at Pazzo's, an Italian place nearby.

Hal knocked on the door minutes later. He looked incredible: casually mussed hair, five-o'clock shadow, expensive shirt paired with dark slacks and Italian shoes. He even smelled wonderful.

"Look at you," she said in admiring tones. "And what is that cologne? I don't remember buying you any."

"It's from my sister, Peg," he said sheepishly. "So the chicks will dig me, she said."

Ugh. For some reason, Shan didn't want to think about other chicks *digging* Hal. He was so sweet. Clueless maybe, but sweet—when you avoided the topic of logic with him. "Well," she said. "Don't put it on your privates, because it'll burn."

He grinned. "Does that little piece of advice come from experience, Shannon?"

"No, I read it in Emily Post. Sit down—" she gestured toward the sofa "—while I grab my bag and a jacket. I'll be right out."

Hal sat carefully on her wild, modern sofa. It was red, shaped like a giant pair of lips. He placed his hands on his knees and looked around, taking in his surroundings. People who came to her apartment for the first time were generally taken aback. In the entryway was a big clock modeled after one of Dali's "Wet Watches," so that it looked as if it were melting.

On the wall behind the lip-shaped red sofa gleamed a giant mirror shaped like a stiletto. And over her mantel, next to a leopard-upholstered chair, hung a series of Warhol "Marilyn" prints. On the floor a white fuzzy rug—a fake bearskin—united the seating area, which surrounded a wide-screen, flat TV.

Hal blinked at her decor and honed in on the plasma television. He emitted a primate-like grunt of delight.

Shannon rolled her eyes when she heard it. And as her eyes rolled, they caught sight of a flash of white. Two flashes, in fact. And they had nothing to do with her rug.

She sucked in her breath with horror. "Hal!" she said sharply.

He jumped. "What!?"

She pointed with a shaking finger. "Get those white socks off your feet right now."

"What's wrong with my socks?"

"Everything!" She flew toward him and grabbed an ankle. "Never, never, *ever* wear white socks with anything but gym shoes. Especially not with dark pants and black shoes."

He shook her off. "Hey! You can't have those. My feet will get cold. There's snow on the ground out there."

"I don't care. The socks come off now or I'll have to resort to violence, do you hear?"

Hal stood up. "Bare ankles will look even stranger."

"You're under arrest by the Fashion Police."

"Oh, yeah? You gonna slam me up against the wall and frisk me, Officer Shane? See if I've got any other illegals on me, like a pocket protector or taped glasses?"

"Put your hands up and step out of the socks, Hal."

"No. I've had enough of being bossed around by you. Now do you want to go to dinner or not?"

Her stomach growled like a Harley. "Yes, but not with a man in dark shoes and white socks. It's… it's…*beyond* dorky, Hal!"

His mouth twisted. "I see. And a former prom princess like you just couldn't be seen with a *dork*. You might lose face in front of your friends, after all."

"Look, we are not in high school anymore. And it might surprise you to know that a prom princess doesn't have it easy, either. I got picked on as the dumb blonde every single day by the algebra teacher, okay? I got humiliated in front of the entire class just for his personal enjoyment."

Hal seemed surprised. "But algebra's so easy," he said.

She counted to ten so she wouldn't smack him. "Not for everybody, it isn't. Now, I'm starving. Are we going to go or not?"

"How about a compromise? I take off one sock, but not the other. That way, we're both a little happy."

"You are a lunatic. That would look weirder than—" She threw up her hands. "You know what? I just don't care. Do what you want, Hal. But you're ruining your new image and all my hard work."

He got up and opened the door for her. "How 'bout I take them off for you later?" He waggled his eyebrows and looked to the fuzzy white rug in front of the fireplace.

She swept past him. "That's another thing we need to talk about, Hal. We've got to put the brakes on anything physical between us."

HAL SCOWLED at Shannon over their shared platters of four-cheese manicotti and shrimp scampi with angel-hair pasta. She'd twisted her mass of blond, curly hair tightly back from her face, and tonight the style accentuated dark shadows that had appeared under her eyes. She wasn't sleeping well—that was obvious. And he knew a way to help her with that….

"What do you mean, put the brakes on anything physical? Does that mean you're done test-driving me? You're moving on to someone more hip? Someone who won't embarrass you in public by wearing white socks?"

"Hal." She reached across the table and put her hand on his. Her green eyes held regret. "No, you're taking this all wrong. I'm not moving on to anybody, okay? The fact is that we need to work together. Our more intimate relationship isn't helping our professional situation."

He pulled his hand from under hers.

She took a gulp of Chianti from her glass and seemed to brace herself before making her next comment. "And you need some practice dating other women. We need to get you out there in the swim of things. Have you go on a few trial runs. I'll set you up with a wire in case you run into any snags, and I'll be right there to guide you."

She sounded like a mom about to put her kid on the school bus for the first time. It pissed him off. "A *wire?* You've got to be kidding me."

"No, I'm not. It will allow me to prompt you out of any awkwardness. And we'll also have a recording of your date to go over the next day, so I can give you pointers."

"Why do you have this kind of equipment, Shannon? Let me guess. You're another Sydney Bristow, with the CIA?" His tone was mocking.

"Funny. No—it's part of my coaching process.

The equipment is pretty standard and easy to come by. It's not something I stole from the set of a Bond movie."

Hal was hurt and didn't bother to disguise it. "So you want me to go out with other women."

"Hal, I like you very much. But it would be healthy for you to see other women."

The big kiss-off. Well, he'd known it was coming, hadn't he? Women like her didn't date guys like him. She'd been slumming. "Oh, I'm all about health."

"Hal, please don't make this harder for me than it is, okay? Do you think I enjoy it?"

Oh, you do revel in your goddess power. You've used and abused the poor, malleable mortal. Now you're finished with him. Time to move on.

"And quite frankly, I'm so mixed up right now that I can't handle seeing anyone."

The old, "it's not you, it's me" speech. How original. Why did I ever think there was anything more to you? "So you're back to the identity crisis, huh?"

"What do you mean, 'back to it?' I never left it. You asked me, Hal, why I got so angry with you? Well, it's because you can't just tell a woman that what she feels isn't logical."

"Shannon, I was only trying to help." *And God knows why. You're not worth the effort.*

"I know that. And it's why I'm sitting here with you. Men just have different ways of problem-solving, I guess. You process and compartmentalize the information and break it down into parts. Women sit on the whole issue, like an egg, until they have a breakthrough."

"Yeah. Whatever." Hal wasn't prepared to extend the evening much longer. He couldn't look at her without feeling a confusing medley of emotions that included affection, sexual attraction, anger, hurt and disgust.

All he knew was that there was a connection between them that could be fostered, if she were willing. But because he didn't meet her requirements in a man—and what were they?—she wasn't willing to give them a chance. She wasn't stupid in the least; she was just shallow. She either could not or would not function too far beneath the surface.

He threw his napkin on the table and stood up. "I'll be right back," he said, heading to the restrooms. He had to pass by the dessert counter on the way, where a petite dark-haired woman gave him a shy once-over.

He pretended not to notice, but then looked back and caught her staring. She blushed. Hal, flattered, gave her a smile. When he returned from the men's room, she was still contemplating the tiramisu and cannoli in the case.

"It's a tough decision, isn't it?" he said to her.

She blushed to the shade of a raspberry and nodded. "Do you come here often?"

He cast a sidelong glance at Shannon, who was watching from their table. "All the time," Hal lied. "I love Italian food. My, uh, sister is in town and I brought her here since it's one of my favorites."

"Well," said the woman, "my name is Megan and I'm here a lot on Thursdays with the girls from work."

"Great," said Hal, nodding. He looked toward Shannon again. She shot him a meaningful stare and pantomimed writing something down. Did she want him to get the check?

"Um, so what's your name, Megan?" Hal said, trying to figure out what his tormentor was trying to communicate.

"Megan," said Megan. "I just told you that."

"Uh, right. Sorry." He stuck his finger into his ear and wiggled it a little. "I, uh, I'm hard of hearing. In the left ear. But not the right."

Megan looked at him strangely. "But you heard my name. You called me by it and then asked me what it was—all in the same sentence."

"Um, yeah. See, I must have read your lips but not processed the information totally…that happens to me sometimes. I was dropped on my head as a child." Hal wondered how on earth to continue this conversation—or how to get out of it. Things weren't going very well. "But I'm okay now. Really."

"That's good." The woman sidled away from him. She raised her eyebrows and flashed him a weak smile. "Well…I'd better figure out what to get for dessert."

"I'm Hal," he said, remembering that he'd forgotten to introduce himself.

"Great." She backed up a couple of steps and stared fixedly at the dessert case.

A waiter behind the case asked, "Can I help one of you?"

Charm, Hal remembered. He recalled the saleslady in the mall. *I'm supposed to smile and compliment. It gets good results.* He showed his teeth to Megan and the waiter, thrust his shoulders back and sucked in his stomach as Shannon had instructed. He put his elbow casually on the case and cocked a hip. "Well, I'd like—"

"Actually," Megan interrupted, "I was here first."

"—to have *her* for dessert. Can you arrange that?" He winked in what he thought of as a charming manner.

The waiter blinked.

Megan rounded on him. "You have a real nerve, you know? And you're starting to give me the creeps. Get away from me!"

This was not the desired result. However, she was serious.

"Right," said Hal, backing away and feeling his neck grow hot. "Maybe I'll just have coffee." Feeling like a giant, neon ass he made his way back to the table. *That went well.*

He slid into the booth opposite Shannon.

"Why didn't you get her number?" she asked.

"Is that what you were gesturing about?"

"Yes. It's helpful, if you want to see someone again, to obtain their contact information."

"Good point. She doesn't want to see me again, though. Apparently I give her the creeps. I think I do need to wear that wire you recommended." And under Shannon's pointed questioning, he related exactly what had happened.

"Hal, honey. You've got to be close to genius IQ. Think about what you're saying before you say it." Her lips quivered as if she were trying not to laugh at him.

"I can think until hell freezes over, but nothing sounds right. I get tongue-tied."

"You're not tongue-tied around me, Hal."

"Yeah, I don't know why that is. Maybe because you ripped my pants off within six hours of knowing me, so let's just say there was no awkward courtship phase."

"Conversation is easy, Hal."

"Not for everyone, it isn't." It struck him that she'd said the same thing about algebra. "Small talk is my algebra," he told her.

She'd been in the process of sipping her wine, but stopped with the glass at her lips, an arrested expression on her face. "Yeah?"

He nodded. "Yeah. I guess everyone has an algebra that they need help with."

She smiled. "Well, here's a formula for you to work with. Everyone likes to talk about themselves. So when you get to an awkward spot in a conversation, or you're trying to start one, ask questions. *Appropriate* questions. Open-ended questions. In other words, you're not going to ask some random woman, 'So, babe, what's your bra size?'"

"That's bad, huh? I think I knew that."

"Yes, that is bad. Your answer will be either a slap in the face, or she'll say, '38D.' In which case you'll have to come up with another question."

"Okay."

"So let's imagine that you're talking with a man at a PR event like the one I'm sending you to in a couple of days."

Alarm bells went off in Hal's head. "Alone?"

"No. I'm going to set you up with a date, and that way we can kill two birds with one stone. It's a benefit for the children's hospital, and you're attending to raise money for the cause *and* raise your profile in the community, which will bring you more business."

"Sounds miserable."

"Hal. It's for a good cause and you'll meet some nice people. Now, here's a scenario—you meet a man there. He says his name is Fred Jones. You need to talk with him, find a connection with him. So you might ask him how long he's been in the community and perhaps what he does for a living. As he tells you, you listen and ask a few more questions about what interests you. He'll give you more information and probably ask you a few polite questions. You hit the conversational ball back and forth. You see how it works?"

"When does it end?"

She laughed and shook her head. "Any time you want it to. You can say, 'Well, Mr. Jones, it's great to meet you. I wish you luck with XYZ. I've got to go say hello to Bob/Judy/Tom. Take care.'"

"Bob/Judy/Tom?"

"Anyone. Or you can say you're going to get a drink, find the facilities, whatever. But you make it clear, politely, that you're ending the conversation. It's really very simple."

"Sounds like a big waste of time. Why do I want to meet Mr. Jones in the first place?"

Shannon closed her eyes. "Because people make the world go 'round. You might be able to help Jones, or he may be able to help you. He might become a close personal friend—you never know. Maybe he's looking for technology like yours, or knows someone who is."

"Hmm. So who is this woman you're setting me up with?"

"She's a friend of my partner Jane's. She's a manager for a department store, her name is Ellen and she's very pretty." Shannon's voice was devoid of emotion, as if she were reading the telephone book to him. She really didn't care. She was just passing him along to someone else without a qualm.

He got angry all over again, even though he told himself it was a waste of time and energy. Her Blondeness didn't give a damn about him. Yet there she sat, across the table, in her tight lime-green sweater and a pair of snug jeans that showcased her ass as though it were a world-cup trophy. A single spiral of hair curled around her left ear, her lips were nude of any color, her large green eyes shadowed.

There she sat, casually dismissing him. And he

wanted her with a fierceness that shocked him. That made him angry, too. Hal tossed back the rest of his own Chianti and set his glass down. "We should be going. I've got work to do."

But he couldn't help himself. He reached across the table and traced the dark circles under her eyes with his index finger. "And you need to go to bed— with me or without me."

18

SHANNON CLIMBED into Hal's Explorer and sank back against its sturdy seat. The truck smelled of leather and carpet shampoo and stability, security. Kind of like Hal the man.

He might wear hideous combinations of clothing and say utterly bizarre things, but he was secure in his own skin, comfortable with himself when he wasn't trying to follow someone else's script. She got the sense, still, that he was humoring her with all this makeover madness. Humoring his mother and sister and attorney, too.

He considered the whole process of—what did he call it?—Suave School ridiculous and only went along with it to get everyone off his back.

While this knowledge didn't make Shannon feel any more successful in life, she had to respect the fact that he liked himself just the way he was. He didn't live for anyone else's approval—or, like her, for their disapproval.

With sudden clarity, she realized that her entire life had been a rebellion against Greenwich and her parents…the people who were not really her parents. The way she dressed, the way she thought, the profession she'd embraced in L.A. Now that rebel streak in her didn't make sense any longer. And it was fading. But she'd been a rebel for so long that *not* being one left her swinging in the wind.

Who was she, if not the flamboyant anti-Greenwich? What role did she now play? She was done being a professional actress—sampling other people's lives. It was time to live her own life.

Now she worked as an image consultant…but was it time to change her own image? She could feel herself changing, but couldn't put her finger on exactly what the changes were. Yes, they had something to do with discovering she was adopted. But they also had to do with Hal, whose sanity and stability attracted her. For the first time ever, she didn't find those qualities boring—not in him. In Hal, they were a challenge.

She slouched farther down into the seat, pulled the belt across her body and secured it. Hal got into the driver's side and fastened his own seat belt. She repressed a smile.

He might look—with the exception of the renegade white socks—like a hip bachelor who'd stepped out of *GQ,* but he still had the habits and lifestyle of a suburban dad working to pay off a hefty mortgage. She found it endearing.

He drove to her apartment and walked her to her door like a Boy Scout. She opened the door and he touched her shoulder, his hand warm through her light sweater.

She turned to find him watching her with an expression she couldn't read. "Hal?"

He dropped his hand.

She wished he wouldn't.

He seemed to see that, because he reached out again, as he had in the restaurant, and touched the dark circles under her eyes.

She closed them at the feel of his fingers on her skin.

He said huskily, "So when I take this woman Ellen out, should I touch her like this?"

Her eyes flew open and he read them before she could stop him. Damn his perception.

"Should I…" He bent his head and his lips brushed hers. "Should I kiss her like this?" And his mouth came down full force on hers.

Unfortunately her response was instantaneous and not something she could control. She opened to him, sagged against him, and kissed him right back.

The Boy Scout had vanished, had been replaced by a wolf. Hal picked her up, walked inside with her and kicked the door closed.

"This has to be the last time," she whispered. "We have to stop this."

He didn't answer her; just kissed her again and set her on the stairs inside her apartment. He moved his hands to her knot of hair and undid it, so that it came tumbling down around her shoulders.

He threaded his fingers through it and she closed her eyes, her scalp tingling.

"You've got bad-angel hair," he said softly. "The color of a halo but the kink of sin." He continued to stroke it and she nuzzled her head against his hands like a cat.

"I want to make love to you until your hair straightens out by itself." He chuckled softly. "Then I want to do it all over again until it goes back the way it was."

"You know, you're pretty damn good at this seduction stuff. At these bedroom lines. I still don't understand what happened to you back there at the restaurant with the little brunette."

Hal looked at her seriously. "She...wasn't you. It was an awkward, artificial situation. And for your information, Shannon, the comments I make aren't lines. But I guess men say things like this to you all the time." He withdrew his hands from her hair and stood up. He shoved his hands in his pockets and looked down at her with that inscrutable expression of his.

She stood up, too. "No, other men do not say the things you say. They're unique. And while you're right that I've been no angel during my lifetime, I haven't been with anyone besides you in a year." She splayed her hands across his chest and kissed him, feeling his nipples grow hard under her fingers as his tongue found hers and mated with it in a slow, intimate dance.

Suddenly he pulled away from her. "Why?"

"I haven't wanted to."

He traced the sensitive flesh and cartilage of her ears and waited. She sighed.

"There was a guy in L.A., a director. An amazing, creative, brilliant man. I fell hard for his work and for him. I thought I was in love."

His hands stilled on her earlobes, but he held them carefully between thumb and forefinger.

"He was casting for the lead in an upcoming film. I won't mention which one, but it's a big deal. You'll start to see trailers for it soon. It will have a star-studded premiere and the whole nine yards." She bit her bottom lip, barely conscious of the fact until Hal tugged at it.

"Hey," he said. "I like that. Don't chew it off."

She released it and expelled her breath. "Yeah. Thanks."

He caressed her jaw and the back of her neck, and she could have cried with the comfort of it. "Anyway. One night we were in bed together, and he offered me the role. It should have been the happiest moment in my life, but I couldn't take it."

"Why not?"

She swallowed. "It was the way that he offered it. So cruel. So mocking. So cynical. He made me feel so cheap."

"What did the bastard say to you?"

She didn't know if she could repeat it to anyone but Jane or Lil, though the words had echoed in her mind for months now.

"Shan, what did he say?"

"He said…since I'd been a hot lay and a…a g-good little cocksucker, I could have the part."

She heard Hal's sharp intake of breath. Then he swore in a highly imaginative and filthy sequence. He pulled her close and kissed her head, hugged her as if he'd never let her go.

"I'm so sorry," he said. "What a son of a bitch."

"I was stunned. And he laughed when he said it, fully expecting me to take the role. The worst part of the whole thing, Hal, was that I almost did. I was tempted! But that sickened me."

He hugged her even tighter.

"Finally I looked at him, and I said, 'I *loved* you, you bastard.'" She put her head on Hal's chest. "And you know what he said? He said, 'Oh, spare me.'"

"I want this guy's name."

She ignored that. "He told me to be on the set in a week, and to save my anger at him for the part. I told him to screw himself. He told me not to be stupid. I left. I never went to the set. And he cast someone else. End of story. I guess I am stupid."

"You're not stupid. You're incredible."

"I'm stupid and I'm a failure. I knew stuff like that went on in the industry. I'd just never seen a Jekyll and Hyde act like that one before. I didn't see it coming. And I didn't have what it takes to make it out there. A tougher woman would have shown up to the set in spite of him."

"In no way, shape or form are you a failure. You have your pride and you're a queen. It took one hundred percent more guts to walk away than it would have to stay. Now give me this guy's name."

"Hal—"

"Just a screen name, on the computer. Something very bad is going to happen to his system."

"No—look, you could get into trouble for that."

"If I got caught. Which I won't."

"Listen to me, okay? It's bad energy. Let it go. I'm letting it go. Every time I tell the story—and this is only the second time, now—the negative force of it lessens. But you're sweet for wanting to avenge me." She smiled at him.

"Come here. You're one in a million, do you know that?"

"Shut up. You're embarrassing me."

"I've got much better ways than that to embarrass you," said Hal. "Naked ways."

"We shouldn't…"

"We should. We definitely should," he told her, and then kissed her again. "You need kissing," he said. "You need lots of it."

He was right.

"Will you take off your clothes so I can kiss the rest of you? Every inch?"

"Yes. If you'll take off those white socks and throw them into the fireplace." She moved to the hearth and flipped a switch to turn on the gas log. It didn't have the same wonderful smell of a real fire, but she didn't have to make a mess to start one, either.

"Deal." Hal followed her and sat on the lip sofa

to pull off his shoes and socks. He had long, sturdy feet. His toes sank into her fake polar-bear rug and he wiggled them in appreciation of the softness.

He sat barefoot and boyish on the giant red lips, and she wanted to eat him up: his kindness and humor and sharp intelligence…but also his sweet goofiness.

Shannon put on some music and swayed to it, turning her back to him and shaking her hair, shoulders and rear to the bass beat. She turned and looked at him over her shoulder, winked at him as he sat mesmerized.

Slowly, still dancing, she peeled off her lime-green sweater, tossed it at him and stretched her arms over her head. She lifted her hair and then let it cascade down her naked back, gyrating for him.

She unhooked her bra and peeked over her shoulder again to find him unblinking, like a cat peering into a fishbowl with evil intent. She laughed.

Still in time to the music, she bent at the waist and stretched down, peering at him from between her own legs. The straps of her bra fell down her arms, leaving her chest bare. She straightened and tossed the bra at him, cupping her breasts as she turned to face him.

Hal's eyes glazed as she dropped her hands to the snap on her jeans and kept on with her striptease. She turned her back on him again and began to work the denim down over her hips until her thong peeked out.

A little more undulating and her cheeks were bare.

Hal looked as if a heart attack were imminent. Finally she stepped out of the jeans entirely and just danced for him in nothing but the thong, which was small and black.

"Where's your pole?" he asked in hoarse tones.

"I think it's right there." She pointed to his tented pants and began to gyrate for all she was worth. She swung it, she spun it, she bumped and she ground. She had a ball, and would have continued if the song hadn't ended and Hal hadn't rushed her like an offensive lineman, throwing his clothes off in the process.

Before she knew it she was under him on the bear-skin rug, and his hands were everywhere she liked best. He dispensed with her thong immediately and threw it into a houseplant. Then he made good on his word of kissing her all over.

He started damn close to the center and radiated outward, trailing his lips from the top of her mons to her belly and the hollow between her breasts. He kissed the swell of those, but not her nipples, while she grew ever impatient. He kissed her collarbone, her neck, her ears, her forehead, her lips.

He kissed her shoulders, her biceps, her wrists—even under her arms, while she struggled to push him away, laughing. "That's disgusting," she complained. "It can't smell good there."

"It does," he promised. "Smells like you." He nuzzled her breasts again, and trailed his mouth down over her ribs, hips and thighs. He made a brief foray to her core again and blew teasingly on the curls he found there while she moved restlessly.

He parted her thighs and kissed the tender skin there, but avoided the more intimate area. He moved down her thighs to her knees and calves, her ankles and feet.

Only then did he start at the top again and pull her toward him. Sitting cross-legged in front of the fire, he coaxed her onto him so that she sat, thighs spread over his, nut to bolt, just barely touching.

He bent his head and just touched the tip of his tongue to her nipple, teasing it gently. Shannon caught her breath and leaned back on her hands. He circled the bud slowly with his tongue and then switched to the other one.

Exquisitely sensitized and barely wet, her nipples now jutted forward aggressively, trying to meet his mouth. When he closed his lips around one and sucked it almost roughly, she cried out and rocked forward, coming into slick contact with his erection. Swirls of pleasure eddied, then faded behind her closed eyelids—until he took the other nipple between his teeth and bit lightly before drawing it into his mouth and kneading both breasts in his hands.

She rocked forward again, slid against him again, and this time he grabbed her bottom, parted her and drove home. The feeling was indescribable as she rose and fell onto him, clinging to his shoulders and barely hanging on as her thighs began to tremble and the wet fullness between them built into a blinding pleasure. Her nipples rubbed against his broad chest, heightening and echoing every sensation she felt at her core. She felt sunshine spreading within her, softly at first and then blazing through every inch of her until she combusted in Hal's arms.

He lay back on the rug, spent, and pulled her on top of him. With Hal warming her front side, and the fire warming her backside, she fell asleep.

19

WHEN SHANNON AWOKE, she was still spooned into Hal. Aside from the floor being a little hard, it was heaven. She felt safe and protected with his big arm wrapped around her; snug. His heart beat steadily against her spine. He stirred against her sleepily and buried his nose in her hair.

She didn't particularly want to move, which surprised her, given the fact that she normally found being clutched annoying. She usually dodged out from under a male arm or leg if it was draped over her. She wasn't a teddy bear.

But Hal didn't mean the gesture as an act of possession. He meant it as a comfort.

She lay there with him for another few minutes, but then peered at her watch. Two in the morning. Carefully she lifted his arm enough that she could slide from under it. He made a sleepy noise of protest, mumbled something, but other than that showed no signs of waking up.

She tucked a blanket around him and crept upstairs to her office in the second bedroom, leaving him naked in front of the fire.

Still nude herself, she sat in her rolling office chair and turned on her computer. She logged on to the Internet and found the site for the Home for Little Wanderers.

She stared at the screen for a long moment, her heart rate spiking. And then she clicked on the link that would put her in touch with someone who could help her. She copied down the address and phone number listed. She'd write to them tomorrow and have them check her file for any correspondence.

Only then would she decide what to do next.

"Shannon?" Hal's voice came from downstairs.

"Coming!" She padded downstairs again. He sat like a big sleepy kid on the rug, legs splayed in front of him. His hair was a disaster and she loved it that way. He blinked at her. "What time is it?"

"Late," she said. She was tempted to just take him upstairs to bed with her, but that would only make things harder tomorrow, when they returned to a professional relationship and nothing more.

He looked a question at her.

"I was just in my office. I'm going to get in touch with the adoption place to see if either of my biological parents has attempted contact or left a letter for me."

He nodded.

"It's called the Home for Little Wanderers. Isn't that quaint?" She half laughed. "And over the years I've grown up to be a Big Wanderer."

"Aren't you done with that? You have a business here now."

She nodded. "Yeah. But who knows…" She found her jeans and climbed into them, then pulled her sweater on inside out. She twisted her hair into its usual knot. "You want something to drink?"

"No, thanks. I guess I'd better head home." He glanced up the stairs, but then shook his head as if reminding himself of something. She wondered what. He, too, found his clothes and pulled them on. He ran a hand through his hopeless hair and grabbed his keys off the console. "Get some sleep, okay?"

She nodded. She walked him to the door and kissed him, probably for the last time. Then she hid behind it so she wouldn't give the neighbors a show when he opened it.

"See you tomorrow?"

She nodded. "Last dress rehearsal before you go out for field testing, Dr. Suave."

"Yeah. That's me. Dr. Suave." He brushed her cheek with the backs of his fingers and touched his lips to hers again. She didn't want him to leave. She was sorely tempted, in fact, to pull him upstairs by the belt and pounce on him in the comfort of her bed. She didn't.

"Good night, Hal."

"Good night."

HAL PEERED at the piece of paper Shannon had given him. She'd scrawled Ellen Finnegan's address on a Post-it note. He was to pick her up at 7:00 p.m. and they'd attend the children's hospital benefit together. Shannon had to go to dinner with another client, but had sworn to put on her headset and join him electronically at precisely 7:45 p.m.

The only problem was that Ellen Finnegan's house number didn't seem to exist on Ellen Finnegan's street. Hal drove it one more time, but number 6429 wasn't there. The numbers stopped with 5400, where there was a dead end. Unless Ellen lived in the ornamental fish pond on that property, or on the community jungle gym, she didn't reside here.

Hal pulled up under a streetlight to examine the Post-it again, and fiddled with the alien earpiece blocking his hearing. The wire inside his shirt felt odd, too, and he had a feeling that the tape holding it in place was going to rip a bald spot in his chest hair when he took it off.

Under the light, he saw to his dismay that he was on Brickton Street in Avon, whereas he was supposed to be on Brickton Avenue in Weathersfield. And he didn't have Ellen's telephone number with him.

Muttering to himself, he yanked a residential map out of his door pocket and dug for his cell phone. A call to Information yielded none, naturally: Ms. Finnegan was unlisted.

Hal found Brickton Avenue in Wethersfield and calculated that it would take him a good forty minutes in traffic to get there. Wonderful. He found Shannon's number on his call list and punched Send. But all he got was her voice mail. By the time he got to her house, Ellen was going to think he was a prize jerk.

He drove and drove, finally squealing up outside

a modest white house with black shutters and a cheerful, flowered Welcome mat. Ellen's face, when she opened the door, was not as hospitable as her rug. A good-looking redhead in a sparkly cocktail dress, she looked pointedly at her watch.

"Hi," said Hal sheepishly. "I'm Hal. I went to the wrong Brickton in the, um, wrong town."

She looked unimpressed. "Isn't this a sit-down dinner?" she asked.

"Uh, yes."

"Then we'd better get moving."

He nodded. *Think, Hal. Charm. Compliments. Smiles. Posture.* "You look nice," he said, standing tall and forcing his shoulders back as they walked to the Explorer. Actually he thought her nose was too long and her dress was too short.

"Thank you." She glanced up at him. "Have you hurt your back? Is it painful to move?"

So much for his posture. Hal downshifted his military strut to his customary amble. "No, no. Just stretching." He opened the passenger-side door for her and she looked in dismay at the height from the street to the running board. Her dress didn't look stretchy, and it was covered with sequins.

"Would you like some, er, help?" Hal asked. "Getting in?"

"Yes, please."

He evaluated the situation, not knowing quite what to do. Finally he put one arm around her shoulders and another under her derriere.

"What are you—?"

He lifted her bodily toward the seat.

"Please be careful of the sequins—*ow!*"

He'd clonked her forehead into the door frame. "Oh, God, I'm sorry! Are you okay?" Hal put her on the seat and tried to get his hands out from under her. But the cuff links that Shannon had insisted he wear snagged on her dress, and due to his lurch when she cried out, his hand was now squarely on her ass.

When he tugged, fondling was unavoidable.

"Get your hands off me!"

It was now imperative that he free himself so that she didn't puncture his gut with her elbow or mace him—or both. Hal pulled back hard and got disentangled from her. Unfortunately so did quite a few sequins and the thread which had held them in place.

Rubbing her head, Ellen saw them and shrieked. "What have you done to my dress?!"

Hal awkwardly volunteered to sew them back on, but was told in no uncertain terms that he wasn't coming anywhere near her with a needle.

"I think this evening is cursed already," she said. "Why don't I just go back inside?"

"Look, Ellen, I'm sorry—honestly I didn't mean to touch you inappropriately. My cuff links got caught on your dress. I'm not quite Mr. Smooth, but I can promise you I'm not normally this much of a disaster. Just give me another chance, okay?"

He had to keep her appeased and in the car: she was his midterm exam. "And only a couple of se-

quins came off. I really don't think it'll be notice-
able at the dinner. Low lighting and all that." He
flashed her an earnest smile.

She seemed to melt under it and calmed down.
"Fine."

He went around to the driver's side, got in and
started the ignition. In a few minutes he had them at
the benefit and turned over the Explorer to a valet
parking attendant.

Another red-jacketed attendant helped Ellen down
without incident, to Hal's relief. He took her elbow as
Shannon had taught him, and escorted her inside the
hotel. He followed a horde of elegantly dressed people
to a grand ballroom filled with round tables and chairs.

Though they were a half hour late, Hal found them
seating at a table immediately and pulled out Ellen's
chair for her. He pushed it in once she'd sat down—
a little too far in, but then he corrected that, afraid
he'd cracked her ribs.

He sat down himself and basked in the glow of her
extremely fixed smile. He was in dire need of a drink
to calm his nerves. "Can I get you something from
the cash bar?" he asked Ellen.

It mildly enraged him that there was a cash bar at
an event that had cost him two hundred and fifty dollars a head, but he couldn't do a thing about it now.

"Yes, please," she said. "A glass of chardonnay."

"No problem," he told her. *And I'm going to find
some Jack Daniel's.* He was in the process of getting
up when an electronic screech split his eardrum. He

jumped, his knee hitting the table. Everything jiggled and clanked, but no other damage occurred. Ellen shot him a scathing glance, but said nothing.

Hal backed away from the table fast. Shannon's voice said into his ear, "Hal, where the hell are you?"

"I'm at a table at the damn benefit. Where are you?"

"Hal, I'm standing next to your place card at your table. You are *not* here."

He began to get a sinking feeling. Place card? He looked around at the tables in the ballroom and saw no reserved seating whatsoever. Then, to his horror, he saw a bride.

"Oh, no. I think we're at someone's wedding reception. We just followed some people in..." He shot a look at Ellen, who'd spied the bride, too. "Listen," he hissed. "This whole date has been a disaster so far! I need your help. I'm not sure it's even salvageable at this point, though."

She sighed. "Hal, start by getting yourselves into the right place. You should be on the second floor in the Chadwick Ballroom. Do you think you can get here or should I send an armed guard with a GPS to escort you?"

SHANNON HAD GROWN TIRED of swinging her boobs over the punch bowl by the time Hal and a sour-looking Ellen made it into the correct ballroom.

"Go to the right," she said into his ear. "Pass three tables and the next one is yours. Don't forget to pull out Ellen's chair."

"Been there, done that, cracked her ribs," was Hal's disconcerting reply.

Ellen must have said, "Excuse me?" or words to that effect, because Hal's next words were, "Oh, nothing. Here we are. Let me—no? I'd be happy to—*okay.* Yes, ma'am, a chardonnay coming right up."

"Hal? Is her dress ripped in the back?" Shannon asked.

"Just a small mishap with the cuff links," he said.

"You're kidding me."

"Wish I were. Now, can you help me salvage this date, or should I just throw cab fare on her dinner plate and run?"

Shannon was torn between the desire to laugh, annoyance that he was screwing up after all her training and a sense of relief that he and Ellen weren't getting along. She'd actually had nightmares about him in bed with Jane's friend.

"Get her that wine, go back to the table and make her feel like the most fascinating woman in the world. Ask her questions, Hal, about her job and her dreams. Compliment her. Above all, listen to her."

"Okay."

He made his way back to the table with their drinks and sat down. Shannon said into his ear, "Congratulations. No white socks." He grinned, and Ellen chose that moment to look up at him. She blinked and stared and blinked again, apparently noticing how good-looking he was for the first time all evening.

"Raise your glass to her," said Shannon. "Toast her."

"So, Ellen. Cheers." He held up his drink. She looked at him uncertainly, but then raised her own.

"To a miserable evening so far, but here's to it getting much better," Shannon said. "And grin that same grin when you say it."

Hal followed her instructions.

Ellen looked startled at first, but then actually laughed.

Excellent. Shannon fed him his next lines and reflected that Jane's friend was pretty, but her nose was too long and her dress was too short. She would have done better to choose something that covered her thighs and showcased her delicate, sexy calves.

She'd mentally cut, highlighted and restyled the woman's hair when she realized that Hal had come to a conversational standstill. "That sounds fascinating," she prompted.

"You have to inventory the entire store, piece by piece?" Hal asked.

Oops.

"That's brutal. How often? Twice a year? You poor thing."

"Good," Shannon told him. "Empathize with her."

"And you do this manually? You know, I'm sure I could devise an automated system for your store and spare you that kind of drudgery. We'd have to incorporate the tags on every item into a computer program."

"Go, Hal!" Shannon exclaimed.

"You already do that? Yes, of course. But what I have in mind is something entirely different. You see…"

And her boy was off and running. She gave him five minutes. "Okay, Hal, enough with the techie talk. Tell her you'll contact her about a program next week, but for this evening, you two should have fun. Ask her if her dress came from her store and tell her how exquisite it is. Ask how she got into retail, etcetera."

He followed her instructions. Shannon heard about ten minutes of "mmm-hmms" and yawned, looking at her watch. "Okay," she said. "Her family. Does she come from a big one?"

Thirty minutes later her feet were killing her, and Hal seemed to be doing fine on his own. "Think you can take it from here, big guy?"

"I agree," Hal said.

"Okay, then. Call me on my cell if you hit a snag." Shannon pulled her earpiece out, dropped it into her evening bag and swiped a crab puff on the way out from a roving waiter.

I hope he doesn't get along with Ellen too well….

An image of Hal kissing Jane's friend flashed through her mind. Her stomach lurched, and the crab puff looked a lot less appetizing. She dumped it into a trash can outside the elevators and went home. When she saw Hal tomorrow, would he belong to another woman?

20

SHANNON STARED blearily at her coffeemaker and got a cup out of the cabinet. She poured her salvation into the cup and reached into the cabinet for the artificial sweetener.

Hal had never called back last night.

It doesn't mean anything, you idiot. Just because he felt he could handle himself without your advice does not signify that he jousted with her too-long nose or got up her too-short skirt.

Shannon refocused on her coffee cup and realized that she was pouring salt into it. Sighing, she dumped it into the sink, rinsed the cup and got another one.

She went through her morning process of getting ready and then scooped up her bag, keys, sunglasses and the stamped letter to the adoption agency, requesting that they contact her about her file.

On the way to work, she stopped at the post office and pulled up to the yawning black rectangular mouth of the outgoing mailbox. She took a deep breath.

Here goes. And Shannon fed her envelope to the box and the unknown.

HAL WAS MUTTERING to himself, his fingers flying over the keyboard of his computer when she walked into his office. He'd managed to make even Enrique's haircut look suspect, and the expensive cashmere sweater she'd made him buy looked as if it had been crumpled like a fast-food wrapper before he'd put it on. If ever a man needed her, Hal did.

"Good morning," she said, looking for any clues as to his previous night's activities. Surely if he'd kissed a woman with that long a nose, she'd have left little round bruises on his face?

"Morning," he said, looking up at her. His fingers still moved on the keyboard. How did he do that?

"Are you ready to go over the basic script from last night?"

"I'm ready to find the source of this damned leak!" He rubbed his face with his hands.

She frowned. "You still haven't found it?"

"No."

"Have you considered the possibility that a former employee of yours is working for him?"

Hal shook his head. "The guy couldn't have gotten this much from a single person—every programmer works on only a small section of my product. No, this is different. And if I don't find out what he's up to and stop him now, he's going to ruin my IPO."

"Isn't your product copyrighted?"

"Yes, but all he has to do is make tiny changes…" Hal threw up his hands. "Nobody has hacked in. Nobody has sent the information out of here on e-mail. I am going to have to do something I never thought I'd do—install hidden security cameras. I've already called to set up the appointment. And it makes me sick."

"I'm sorry."

"Yeah, me, too." He looked far too stressed to have spent the night having screaming sex with another woman. She felt bad for him. She also felt relieved.

Why can't I be a nice person and just wish the best for him?

"Well. We should go over your date. And we should get you prepared for tomorrow's interview with *Business Weekly.*"

He sighed. "All right."

She questioned him about developments with Ellen and was unaccountably thrilled to learn that he hadn't even kissed her good-night. "Why not?" she asked. "Things were going very well at that point, right?"

Hal shrugged. "Yeah. But I didn't want to kiss her. She's not you."

Shannon looked down at her notepad and did her best to assume a severe expression. "You have to move on, Hal. We both do. You'll graduate from Suave School very soon, and you'll have dozens of women lining up to date you."

He didn't look excited at the prospect.

Her heart danced a little jig. She told it to break a leg. *You're just looking for someone to hang on to in this time of uncertainty. Hal is not for you. Now let him go. You're not being fair to him, otherwise.*

She grilled him in detail about the rest of his evening. Yes, the conversation had gone fine. He'd been able to be himself. Yes, he'd actually made small talk with some complete strangers and not offended them or bored them to tears. He had the business cards to show for it. And yes, if he had to, he could make an appearance at another one of these boring social events and manage not to embarrass himself.

"Good." Shannon nodded. "Now, the next time a woman needs help getting into your truck, you offer her your hand. You don't pick her up like a sack of potatoes and grab her ass—even accidentally."

"Roger that," said Hal.

"You always make sure you have a correct address and directions before you pick up a date. You try not to be more than five minutes late."

"Check."

"And make sure you find the right ballroom next time."

"Got it."

They moved on to the interview preparations. "Reporters," Shannon warned him, "are crafty. They want to get a good angle for a story, and they'll use anything that comes out of your mouth. Your job is to stay on target with the message that *you* want them to report. That means sometimes not answering their questions directly and pulling the focus of the interview in an alternate direction. This goes for either print or television, okay?"

He nodded.

"In service of getting your message across, you don't want to distract the reporter or your possible audience from that message with fidgeting, odd mannerisms or strange clothing. Even a shiny nose can be a distraction on television. You want to look relaxed, but professional."

"Uh-huh."

"In preparation for the interview tomorrow, I'm going to put you on camera today and work with you on various things. We're going to plan everything down to the last detail—even a couple of jokes. We'll especially focus on what to do about surprise questions. Remember, the reporter's job is to knock you off balance and off message. Your job is to not allow this."

She hauled him into the conference room where she'd set up a video camera and two chairs. They went over and over the basics, then she turned on the camera and played reporter.

"Mr. Underwood, you started a technology company out of your college apartment at the age of nineteen. You specialized in programming for the insurance industry, because your father worked as an actuary. The business was so successful that you never finished your studies. Do you regret that?"

"Not at all," Hal said calmly. "I read widely on my own, and because what I do is so specialized and customized, the lack of a diploma has never hurt me."

"Certainly not financially, as you're about to make an IPO. What can you tell us about the products that

Underwood Technologies offers? Do you do quoting for insurance companies? Issue policies?"

"No, actually, Shannon, what we do is a little different. We do risk/catastrophe modeling for such events as hurricanes, floods, tsunamis and earthquakes. We help the company understand what their exposure is by geographic area, making an estimate of their losses in the event of a natural disaster."

"Tell me more, Hal."

"Well, if a company knows what its exposure is, then they are better able to set their rates and manage their book of business. They are able to estimate what their reinsurance costs will be—"

"How can you accurately predict what a natural disaster will do?"

"We merge actual data on previous disasters with mapping data for a given geographic area...in plain English, we can give a range of possibilities for the company to be prepared for. The company then goes and buys an insurance policy from a bigger company to protect it against catastrophic loss under those circumstances."

She asked him several more questions about his software and then threw in a couple of monkey wrenches. "Hal, how can you be sure that your software makes accurate predictions?"

"We have a proven track record and can demonstrate it mathematically. If you put correct data into the program, you are guaranteed an accurate prediction. Of course, we don't have a crystal ball, Shannon. A prediction is an estimate. But we give our clients the best estimate out there."

"Recently there have been rumors in the business press of a competitor with a similar software. How does that compete with yours?"

Hal stared levelly at her and then the camera. "I'm confident that when put side by side with any competitor, Underwood Technologies's software is superior in terms of user-friendliness, speed and accuracy."

"And what about price?"

"Just remember that you get what you pay for. Saving ten dollars today could cost you thousands if there's a bug in your software."

"Are you saying there's something wrong with your competitor's program, Hal?"

He faced the camera and smiled confidently. "Of course not. But I *am* in the business of forecasting."

"Thank you, Hal."

Shannon got up and turned off the camera. Then she slowly clapped her hands. "You may still be having problems in the dating arena, but other than that? You're about to graduate from Suave School, babe. Congratulations."

HAL'S INTERVIEW with *Business Weekly* went spectacularly well, if he did say so himself. But Shannon said so, too, and beamed at him from the sidelines as if he were five years old and had succeeded in gluing macaroni and dried beans to a sheet of construction paper in art class.

Behind the scenes, he'd been doing a lot more than that. While it had finally sunk in that he couldn't stop the leak from occurring, what he could do was insert bugs in his own software. Whoever stole information would also steal big headaches.

And when Underwood Technologies made a sale to a new client, he would simply remove the bug from the program before giving it to them.

Hal was pretty happy with this solution, which bought him more time to track the source of the theft.

What he was not happy about was his last assignment from Shannon. "Choose a woman," she commanded him. "And ask her out on a date."

He didn't really want to ask any of the women he knew on a date. And even less did he want to go to a bar, park or coffee shop to pick up a random one. The woman he wanted was Shannon.

He was reviewing a contract when Tina undulated into his office with yet another stack of handwritten phone messages. "Hi, Hal." She winked at him. "Lookin' good!"

He thought about telling her that flirting with him was inappropriate and taking messages by hand was inefficient. But truth to tell, she wasn't that hard on the eyes in her tight, baby-blue sweater and an equally tight brown suede miniskirt. In fact, was that part of her bra peeking out of her neckline? Hmm. Interesting.

Hal needed a date. She acted as though she wanted one. He didn't think about any awkwardness later. He just took the path of least resistance.

"Tina, do you have plans tomorrow? I was thinking of trying that new seafood place downtown."

She looked at him and giggled. "Well, sure, Hal. Okay."

"Pick you up at seven-thirty?"

"Fine. I'll give you directions to my apartment."

Good idea. Include the town.

Tina gave him an excellent view of her cleavage as she placed the messages on his desk. She winked at him and exited the room.

The chicks were digging him. He had a date. This was part of the reason he'd gone through all the stupid, painful makeover crap. So why wasn't he more excited?

21

HAL'S EARPIECE tickled and made his ear feel as if it were clogged. "Pulling up to the door," he said to Shannon.

"You in the right city?"

"Funny." He got out and headed upstairs to the second floor of Building D. "About to ring the doorbell."

"I'm breathless with anticipation."

Hal rolled his eyes and leaned on the little white button to the right of Tina's beige apartment door.

She opened it and he almost keeled over from perfume inhalation. Whew! She'd poured a pint of something over herself. Shrill, staccato barking assaulted his ears from somewhere behind her.

"Hi, Hal." Her eye-popping silver dress had been painted on her, and highlighted every personal crevice. Every swell. Every not-so-swell.

"Hi, Tina." He produced a smile and tried not to stare. "Your dress is really something." So were the four-inch dangling rhinestone earrings and the four-inch spike-heeled silver sandals. He didn't quite know how to break it to her that they were going to a chowder house.

"Thanks!" She snapped her gum. "Let me just kiss Binkie goodbye and we can skedaddle."

"Who the hell is Binkie and what is Tina wearing?" Shannon said into Hal's ear.

"Later," he muttered.

Binkie turned out to be a white toy poodle in a pink plastic kennel. Hal did not find him in the least kissable, but Tina assumed the position of a large, sparkly frog and puckered up to the grille of his pink palace.

Since the fabric of her dress had stretched to the sheerness of plastic wrap, Hal discovered to his dismay that Tina wore not a stitch underneath. He hoped fervently that she would keep her legs crossed at all times in the chowder house.

Kiss complete, Tina straightened, teetered dangerously on the spike heels and clutched his arm for balance. He righted her and escorted her to the truck. Unlike Ellen, she didn't seem put off by the height of the wheel base, and she scrambled up without any help. Hal gave thanks to the spandex gods that her dress didn't explode off her body and went around to the driver's side.

Dinner was full of giggles, "shut *ups*" and "no ways." Hal pretended to be fascinated by his receptionist, and laughed loud and often. He remembered to be complimentary and charming. He made her feel like the only woman in the world. But his performance was not for her benefit. It was for Shannon's. He wanted to show her that he wasn't hopeless; she'd taught him well.

"So, I'm doing okay, huh?" he said, when Tina undulated off to the ladies' room.

"You're on fire, buddy." Shannon's voice sounded flat. "You're becoming an accomplished flirt."

"Thank you," he said, gratified.

The evening wore on, and he disguised his extreme boredom and distaste. Tina ate clam chowder, fish tacos, French fries and a lot of ketchup. She drank a quantity of sweet pink wine: three generous glasses. She also had decaf coffee and a large wedge of pie.

Hal ate lobster bisque and mahimahi over rice. He had one beer, real coffee and no dessert. "Well," he said, finally. "It's getting late."

She sparkled at him and reapplied her lipstick at the table. "My favorite time." She winked.

"Heh, heh." Hal paid the tab and escorted her out to the Explorer. She sat a little too close to him, and kept touching his shoulder while he drove.

"Well, here we are!" He pulled up to her apartment building and shifted into Park. "It's been a wonderful evening, Tina," he said as sincerely as he could. "Thank you."

"Oh, it *has*."

"I'll, uh, walk you to your door." He did.

She unlocked it and turned to face him.

Uh-oh. What the hell did he do now?

She angled her head, clearly expecting a kiss.

I really, really don't want to kiss her. But is it rude not to? Will I hurt her feelings?

"Oh, Hal. You're just so cute and shy," Tina said. Then she launched herself at him with both hands and swung from his neck until he bent his head. She suctioned onto him and stuck her tongue into his mouth.

"Mmmmmwhummmm," said Hal, revolted.

"Put your hands on my titties, like this, Hal," she said, breaking away and grabbing his hands. "I know you've fantasized about it." She clamped his hands to her breasts.

"Er…"

"Squeeze, baby, squeeze!" She felt behind her for the doorknob, turned it, and tugged him inside.

"No, really—"

Tina pushed him onto her sofa and climbed astride him. She pulled the straps of her dress down to expose her gigantic bosom, and the nipples stared him in the eyes accusingly.

Hal blinked and goggled at them. No, this was… this was *bad.* They were like something out of *Mad* magazine, and he wished she would put them away. "Tina, I can't—"

"Oh, Hallie." She stuffed one into his mouth.

"Mmmffffwha."

Tina pulled his shirt out of his waistband, running her hands underneath the fabric to his…

"Oh, my God!" she hollered.

Wire. *Oh, shit, the wire!*

SHANNON LISTENED in growing distress as Tina and Hal kissed. Even though she told herself that this would have happened eventually on one of his dates, did it have to happen on this one? And with *Tina?* At "Squeeze, baby, squeeze!" Shannon ripped the earpiece out and threw it onto the moldy carpet of the beemer. Hal had disappeared into the tramp's apartment, and she could obviously call it a night. No way was she going to offer him pointers while he had sex with his receptionist.

Men were despicable. They'd hump anything with two tits and a hole. She started the car and took off like a bat out of hell. The night air was heavy with impending moisture, but she didn't bother putting the top up until she got home.

"TINA," said Hal, "I can explain—"

She burst into tears. "You know everything!"

"Huh? Well, not quite," he admitted modestly.

"You're working with the FBI! You brought in the police!"

"*What?*"

"I was forced to do it," she sobbed, rivulets of inky mascara running down her cheeks, "blackmailed."

"Do what?"

"He gave me the little memory stick thingy, and instructions on what to do."

Light dawned on Hal. "Greer Conover."

"Yes, him. The rat. He said he'd skin Binkie alive and make a hat out of him. He said he'd have my granny kicked out of the nursing home. He said—"

Hal tugged her dress up so that she was decent and

got her off his lap. "Sounds like he said a lot of things."

"He did. And he took naked pictures of me that night we went out. He said he'd put those on the Internet and make sure my dad saw them."

Paris Hilton, eat your heart out.

"Greer," Hal told her, "has always been such a friendly guy."

"He's an asshole," she sobbed. "With a pencil dick."

Hal choked.

She wiped at her eyes with the back of her hand. "You're going to fire me, aren't you?"

No sense in lying. "Well, yes. But I'll give you a very nice severance package if you'll cooperate with a police investigation."

SHANNON SLAMMED into her apartment and sank down onto her leopard upholstered chair. The many faces of Marilyn stared at her as her tears came, hot and humiliating and unwelcome.

Outside, the rain started, too, beating steadily down on the roof and splattering the windows in cooperation with gusts of wind.

The Marilyns witnessed her realization: that she'd gone and fallen in love with Hal Underwood.

She'd turned him into the hot guy that all the chicks would dig. But now that she'd transformed him, she'd give anything to have him all to herself, just the way he was the day she'd met him. Shaggy, baggy and awkward. Sweet.

What had she done to him? She'd turned him into the kind of guy who banged his receptionist on a whim. A guy who knew the power of his looks and money to ignite female fantasies.

The thought of him with his hands on Tina's breasts sickened her. She felt bile rising in her throat as she looked at her fake bearskin rug. The rug where he'd so tenderly made love to her the other night.

Shaking, she hurtled toward it and rolled it tightly, wishing she could set it on fire or ram it down the garbage disposal or flush it down the toilet.

She settled for cramming it into the coat closet, where she wouldn't have to look at it.

Hal could have at least thought of her for the split second it took to remove the microphone. He must have had to anyway, so Tina wouldn't find the wire.

She imagined the whole scenario.

Squeeze, baby, squeeze! And Hal would have obliged with gusto. He might even have pinned Tina's wrists over her head so that she wouldn't find his secret; gotten excited over her willing captivity…

But he'd have gone into the bathroom, ripped off the equipment and stuffed it into his pants pocket. Then he'd have ditched his clothes and come out naked.

As for Tina…she'd have been a one-step strip. No way had she had on anything under the tacky piece of plastic wrap she'd worn.

Stop thinking about it. Just stop it! Shannon searched for anything that would block the images from her mind. Vodka. She had a bottle in the freezer. She walked into the kitchen, opened the freezer door and stared at the almost-full bottle. Icy cold, opaque with frost, it beckoned her. She slammed the door on it.

Too many people in L.A. had tried to block their problems that way. Altering the mind didn't alter the reality to which you returned.

She put on loud music instead: an old, punk-inspired, angry Red Hot Chili Peppers album, which fit her mood perfectly. She turned it up to screaming level, knowing that she'd have complaints from the neighbors any moment, though she hoped the on-slaught of rain would kill some of the sound.

Within five minutes, she heard pounding on her door, and sighed. While she wanted to ignore it or tell Mrs. Parker—it had to be Mrs. Parker—to do some-thing biologically impossible, she couldn't.

Shannon turned down the music, opened the door and found a wet Hal on the other side.

"Can you believe it?" he exclaimed.

She stared at him scathingly. "That you got laid? Here's a news flash for you, Hal. That woman prob-ably humps her own doorknobs. So don't be so proud of yourself."

His jaw dropped open.

"Congratulations. You've graduated from Suave School. I'll send you a bill. Now get out."

"Shannon, you don't understand—"

"I understand perfectly. She fell into your lap all wet and juicy and you couldn't say no."

"That's not what happened at all—"

"Squeeze, baby, squeeze!" she shouted at him. "I was listening to the whole thing, remember? So don't lie to me, no matter how well you've learned to do it. I taught you, after all. That's the sick part."

Hal started to look angry himself. "I'm not lying to you. But what the hell are you so upset about, anyway? You also taught me to go out with other women, Shannon! I was supposed to move on, remember? I wasn't cool enough for you, with my white socks and all. So what right do you have?"

"None," she shouted. "None at all. Except that I thought you were still this pure, cerebral guy, someone better than that. And I'm sorry that I changed you, because I liked you a lot better before!"

Shannon put both hands on Hal's chest and shoved, knocking him off balance.

"Is that right?" he said, his soulful blue eyes snapping with temper. He put his hands on her door frame and leaned in toward her, his breath hot on her face.

"Well, I've got a news flash for you, too, babe. You're capricious as hell, impossible to please and I'm done pandering to your every whim. Don't you dare pull this territorial crap when you don't want me yourself. Got it? And you go ahead and send me that bill. I'll include a hefty bonus for you to stay away from me."

And Hal walked away without a backward glance. His slouch was gone and for once his posture was perfect in the pouring rain. It didn't look awkward or assumed. Rage became him.

Shannon took one step after him and then stopped. She went inside, curled up on her lip sofa and sobbed herself to sleep.

22

HAL TRIED to get control over his temper as he drove away from Shannon's apartment. The weather was horrendous and fit his mood to a tee. Cold spring rain sluiced down his windshield and increased the night gloom.

It was late and he was in for a long day tomorrow, filing the police report with Tina.

Though he had insisted that she find another job, he'd promised his receptionist that he would not allow anyone to turn Binkie into a hat or turf her granny out of the nursing home. As for Greer Conover's nude pictures, he'd do his best to see that they weren't published, but he couldn't guarantee anything.

He supposed he could understand why Shannon thought he'd slept with Tina. She'd heard what sounded like a highly enjoyable date, followed by a definite come-on, a sexual command and slurping noises.

If he'd been in her situation, he probably would have thrown off his earpiece, too. Who wanted to listen to a friend…no, a lover…engage in naked acrobatics with somebody else? Just the thought of Shannon with another man made him crazy. But then, Hal had been stupid enough to fall in love with her.

She was just being unreasonable and territorial. She'd certainly given no indication of returning his feelings.

But what really pissed him off was her accusation that he'd lied to her.

Hal might be a workaholic with antisocial tendencies. He might be competitive and not have much fashion sense. But he had never been a liar, and if she didn't know that by now then she wasn't as bright as he gave her credit for being.

Hal pulled into a convenience store along Route 4 in Farmington, and got gas. He swiped his credit card through the machine, pulled out the nozzle and twisted open the cap to his tank. He inserted the nozzle and began fueling up.

Something didn't make sense to him. Shannon was supposedly too cool to care if he slept with another woman. Wasn't she? Hal applied male logic to the issue.

Since she had gotten so upset, either she wasn't as cool as she claimed, or she did, in fact, care for him. Or maybe both.

He frowned. They'd had a fight about his male logic before, however. Male logic and female logic didn't work the same way, although of course male logic was superior and always would be.

He finished with the gas and sealed his tank.

After climbing back into the Explorer and hitting the road again, he decided he needed a female perspective on the situation, and called Peg from his cell phone.

"Whah? 'Lo?"

He'd obviously woken her up. "Peg, it's Hal. I know it's late."

"Is it Mom? Oh, my God—is she okay?"

"Mom's fine. I'm having woman trouble."

"You can't be having woman trouble. You're dating your computer."

"I am having woman trouble," he repeated. "And I need your advice."

"You mean you got laid?"

"Yes."

Peg praised God, all His angels and Shannon Shane, Image Consultant. Then she demanded to know what poor girl had had the bad judgment to sleep with him.

"Shut up for a minute, Peg, and answer this question. If a woman claims you should date other people, but freaks when she thinks you slept with someone else, what's up with that?"

"Well, duh, Hal. She's jealous."

"What if she's too cool to be jealous?"

"Nobody is too cool to be jealous. And maybe she just didn't realize before that she had a thing for you."

"Before when?"

"Before you slept with someone else! Wow, that means you got laid twice. We should alert the press."

"I didn't sleep with anyone else."

"I'm so confused," said Peg. "Hal, it's after midnight. Can this wait until morning?"

"I guess so."

"Good. Because…oh, no. Now I'm going to have nightmares about my brother having sex. Gross! And I was having the best George Clooney dream, too."

"Well, pardon me, Peg. I didn't mean to disgust you or interrupt your rendezvous with El Cloon."

"He's wearing a Speedo," she said dreamily. "Small. Yellow. Stretchy."

"Ugh."

"Banana-flavored."

This was far too much information, even in a fantasy. "And on that note, I'm outta here, Peg!"

"G'night."

He hung up. Was it possible that Shannon cared for him? Or was she just a spoiled, fickle woman who wanted to drive him crazy?

He thought about the things she'd confided to him: her issues with her adoption and her experience with the director in L.A. Somehow, he couldn't just write her off. But he didn't exactly feel like sending her flowers right now.

He drove home through the rain and let it cool him down a little. He thought about what he could do to get through to her, to make her listen to him, believe him about Tina. He thought about what he could do to reach her cool, emotionally scarred, L.A. heart.

LILIA ANSWERED the phone at Finesse when Shannon called in.

"What's wrong, hon?"

She hated to lie to her friends, and it was colossally lame for her to not go in today, but she couldn't drag herself out of bed. "I don't feel well. Stomach virus. I only have two appointments in the afternoon, and with your help, I'll reschedule them both."

"My help meaning that you've forgotten your Palm Pilot again?"

"How did you know?"

"It's in the kitchenette next to the fruit bowl."

Shannon produced a weak laugh.

"How are you going to stay organized when you can't even remember to take your Palm Pilot with you?" Lil's tone was mock-severe.

"I've got a mind like a steel trap," Shannon mumbled.

"You've got a mind like a steel drum," Lil corrected. "Empty and echoing."

"Thanks for the pep talk." She got the client phone numbers from Lil and told her, "I'll be in tomorrow."

"Okay. Feel better, sweetie."

Shannon hung up the phone and stared at the abstract painting on her bedroom wall for a while. As usual, it promised the keys to the creative universe and failed to deliver. She closed her eyes again, couldn't fall asleep, and reluctantly swung her legs out of bed.

The hardwood floor was cold and rather dusty. If she were a person who cared more, she'd vacuum. But she couldn't bring herself to care.

She shuffled downstairs in her pj's, discovered that she'd run out of coffee and almost bawled over the fact, which was just pathetic. If she ordered a couple of gallons of coffee and three dozen doughnuts, would Krispy Kreme deliver? Doubtful.

Shannon drank a cup of ice water and ate the three stale fortune cookies in her cabinet, grimacing over the little paper predictions inside.

"You will be successful beyond your wildest dreams." *Well, obviously. Just look at me.* She tossed that fortune into the trash.

"You will be lucky in love." *Yup. A vibrator never lies to you or cheats on you.*

"Pull your head out of your ass." *Oh, perfect.* She laughed. This one was in Jane's handwriting, and Shannon spent a few minutes trying to figure out how she'd gotten the tiny piece of paper out without cracking the cookie.

Obviously a corner of it must have been peeking out, and she'd just tugged on it until it came free. Then she'd written her own version and stuffed it inside. Yup—there was glue residue on the cellophane wrapper.

Breakfast consumed, Shannon flopped onto the lip couch and explored the offerings of daytime television. Finally she muted the volume and just watched various people run around and make gestures with their lips moving. The one thing she refused to do was think about Hal.

At eleven, she ordered a supreme pizza. When it arrived, she systematically picked off every black olive on the gooey disk and then ate the entire thing while her stomach stretched tighter and tighter.

She passed another hour in extreme regret for her piggyness, feeling bloated and sick.

During the hour after that, she popped cherry-flavored antacids and groaned a lot. And when the soaps came on, she watched two female stars scheme, bitch and then tug each other's hairpieces off in a public fountain while their wet designer clothing stuck to their breasts.

Come to think of it, she'd auditioned for the role of one of their daughters—the one who'd driven off a cliff in the second episode of the season, leaving her illegitimate newborn and a mysterious buried box behind.

Shannon was trying to remember what had been in the box when her doorbell rang and she had to maneuver her bowling ball of a stomach off the couch to see who was there.

A guy from an overnight delivery service stood outside with an envelope. She signed for it, thanked him and accidentally burped before closing the door. She looked down at the return address and her pepperoni-encrusted heart stopped.

The envelope was from the Home for Little Wanderers. She stared at it while her heart did a backflip and then launched into a tap sequence. Slowly she sat down and pulled the cardboard tab to open the packet.

There were two letters inside. One was from the adoption agency. The other was in a plain, white, sealed envelope.

The cover letter was simple and to the point.

Dear Ms. Shane,

Thank you for contacting the Home for Little Wanderers regarding your adoption. We have searched for and found your file, which contained the following sealed letter from your biological mother. It was her wish that should you ever require more information about her, we would forward this to you.

If you have further questions or concerns, please do not hesitate to contact us and we will do our utmost to help you.

Sincerely yours...

Shannon stared at the white envelope and swallowed. The pizza roiled in her stomach. She went to the kitchen, got a knife, and took a deep breath before slitting open the seal.

My dear daughter,

Please know that I love you and have loved you from the moment I knew you were inside me. Though I have not been able to hear you say your first words or see you take your first steps; though I have not been able to share your life and watch you become the beautiful young woman that I know you are; I hope that you can feel my love from afar, for the circumstances of my life do not permit me to meet you.

Giving you up for adoption was the hardest decision I have ever had to make. I struggled with the dilemma every month that I carried you and for the precious month that I truly mothered you. Please understand that I didn't make the decision lightly, and that it took more from me than I could ever hope to give you.

My dear, I could not support you. Taking you home to my parents was not an option. Marrying your biological father was not an option. I was told of a wealthy childless couple who wanted you desperately and could give you everything that I could not: constant attention and nurturing, a comfortable home, good schooling and a happy life.

Please understand that I made my choice, in the end, for you. I still remember your sweet, milky baby scent, your tiny fingers and the way they clung to mine, and the way you nestled in my arms. You will be with me in my heart until the day I die.

All my love,
Your Mother

Shannon read and reread the letter, her tears bathing the slanted, loopy handwriting. Her mother hadn't signed a name, hadn't left an address—not even a phone number or e-mail.

The circumstances of my life do not permit me to meet you. What circumstances? But no details appeared. No way to contact her in order to ask them. The letter was tender, loving, but it was also a very sweet entreaty to be left alone. It was clear that Shannon wasn't welcome to turn up on her biological mother's doorstep for a long-awaited reunion.

This was the type of information she'd feared. A double rejection. The stiff-arm treatment, no matter how gently presented. Her mind flooded with a thousand questions, Shannon turned her gaze back to the silent television and watched the actors and actresses go through the motions of life.

She felt suspended and weightless, as though she were underwater and unable to move with any urgency. She watched a woman slap a man, a snake menace a child, an executive get into an elevator. None of it meant anything or triggered any emotion. Once the final tear had fallen on the letter in her lap, she went numb.

23

SHANNON AWOKE to sunshine streaming through her bedroom window. Clearly it was there to mock her. How dare the sun shine when she'd managed to chase away the guy she loved and turn him into a jerk? How dare the sky be blue and birds chirp when her own biological mother didn't want to meet her?

She staggered out of bed and headed toward the bathroom, where it was hard for her to even find the energy to brush her teeth. She squeezed out some toothpaste onto her brush and did so anyway. She scrubbed at a back molar and glared at her reflection. She had sheet marks on her face and her hair…yikes. She looked like a cross between Einstein and Ozzy Osbourne, and didn't much care. She put herself on automatic pilot and got through the shower, fueled only by the knowledge that if she wanted coffee, she had to go out for it.

Minutes later she stood in front of her closet, discombobulated. She did not want to wear her orange leather jacket. She did not want to wear her jean jacket with the hand-embroidered Chinese dragon on it. She obviously would not wear a black cocktail dress to work.

No jeans, though she longed for them—not professional. Red suit? Yeah, right. Hip navy waitress dress? Maybe. Very retro. Nope. She didn't feel retro today, or hip, come to think of it. Black pencil skirt with two-inch back vent? Too confining.

At last she chose low-slung, wide-legged wool pants with a faint pinstripe. She stuck a leg into them as the phone rang, and hobbled to the bedside table to answer it, wondering what she was going to pair the slacks with.

She normally enjoyed getting dressed in the morning—she considered it costuming. Her clothes projected whomever she chose to be that day. It was fun.

"'Lo?" She stuck her other leg in, pulled up the pants and felt the zipper brush her backside. She looked down to find a pregnant pooch of fabric at her waist. *Brilliant. I just put my slacks on backward.*

Next she'd forget a top altogether and go to work in her bra.

"Shan? Are you feeling better?" Lilia, bless her, had called to check up on her.

No. I'm not sure I'll ever feel better. "Yes, I'm fine. I'll be in the office in about half an hour."

"Okay. By the way, Hal Underwood just came by. He dropped off an envelope for you."

Her heart lurched. She told it to right itself. *Hal is a goat.* "Weird. I haven't sent him a bill yet."

"Kudos, Shan. He looks incredible."

Yeah, kudos. "Well, I couldn't have made him look worse, right?" She forced out a brittle laugh.

"I think he was very disappointed that you weren't here."

"Bummer," Shannon said lightly. "Well, I've got to finish drying my hair. Sorry I'm running late. I fell asleep without setting the alarm. Bc there soon."

ALL DAY LONG, she refused to open the envelope. It was brown, nine by twelve inches, and definitely contained more than a check. She glared at it. Was it bad poetry? A ream of insults? Who knew. She was done opening mysterious envelopes. They never contained good news.

She pulled herself together to meet with three clients, sent PR packets out to two others and scheduled a speaking engagement. She dredged up a smile and some friendly words for Janna, the high school girl who was "paying" for her consultations by helping with direct mail.

She had blossomed with a little guidance and no longer hid her face behind her hair. She even smiled in spite of her braces—which would come off in less than a year.

Still, Shannon had the sensation that she was functioning underwater, in slow motion, and that nothing she accomplished meant anything. She ate a giant chocolate bar for lunch, ignoring the raised eyebrows of Jane and Lil.

She was slumped in her chair at the end of the day,

aimlessly playing solitaire on her computer and still ignoring the envelope, when her partners invaded her office. Lil picked up her purse—dropping Shannon's Palm Pilot into it—and Jane held out her raincoat.

Shannon squinted at them and stuck her lip out. "I don't wanna. If I drink cosmos, I'll get all weepy and pathetic."

"Yes," said Jane. "That would be the point. You need to talk about it."

"About what?"

"God, grant me patience. About whatever is turning you into a mope. It doesn't take my degree in behavioral psych to figure out that you are depressed and repressing your feelings. Now suck your lip in, sweetie, and stand up."

"Leave me alone," she begged.

"We left you alone yesterday," said Lil.

"It's not good manners to pry," Shannon said, in a last-ditch attempt to keep sulking alone.

"Shan, you're as rude as they come," Lil retorted, "so I just figure I'm making you feel at home."

Shannon produced a weak grin and let them bully her out the door. They went just down the road to Max a Mia, where her friends set a cosmopolitan in front of her in short order. They also ordered appetizers, since she'd need something to soak up the alcohol after her unhealthy lunch.

"Speak," said Jane. "My brilliant powers of deduction tell me that this all has something to do with Hal Underwood."

"So do mine." Lil nodded. "And I notice that you still haven't opened his envelope."

"I hate him," Shannon said by way of explanation. "But it's my own fault." She picked up her glass and let some of the vodka roll over her tongue. "That's the worst part. I told him to date other women, so he did."

Jane made a sympathetic noise.

"But I didn't tell him he should sleep with his tacky receptionist right after we…" She took another sip. Then she said to Lil, "You want a fake bearskin rug?"

Her friend shuddered. "Absolutely not."

"Just checking." She turned to Jane. "You?"

"No, thanks. Especially not if it has butt-prints on it. But it's, uh, generous of you to offer."

"Yeah."

Jane and Lil looked at each other. "Okay. So you told him to move on, and now you're mad at him for moving on. That makes sense."

"I know." Shan looked at them woefully. "And then he lied about it and said that he didn't sleep with her!"

"How do you know he's lying?"

"Because she clamped his hands onto her boobs, dragged him into her lair and I heard them kissing through the microphone. *Ugh!* And then it took him forever to show up at my apartment later to crow about it. Like, 'Hey, teach, do I get a gold star for that?' Unbelievable!"

"That's bad."

"Then the jerk tells me that he didn't sleep with her and gets mad at me!"

"You're sure he's lying?"

"Yes."

"Well, then you're well rid of him." Jane's steady brown eyes held regret.

"Yup." Shannon's lip trembled. "But somewhere along the way, I fell for him. And I never thought he was a liar."

Lilia reached over and hugged her. "I'm sorry."

"But it gets worse. You know how I made the decision to see if my birth mother left anything in my file? Well, she did. A letter. And it said she loves me, but I can't meet her because the 'circumstances of her life' don't permit it. The letter may as well have said 'Don't bother me.'"

"Oh, Shannon." Jane squeezed her hand.

"And it's like a double rejection. First, she gives me up. Second, she doesn't want to see how I've turned out. I have this overwhelming urge to…to hunt her down and *force* her to see how I've turned out! The letter was loving, but it also makes me angry."

"That's completely understandable." They all sat in silence for a moment, while the buzz of restaurant noise went on around them. Glasses clinked, laughter carried over from other booths, another song began on the sound system.

Finally Jane said, "About the letter. There are all kinds of possible scenarios. Your birth mother is probably married now. She may never have told her husband that she had a baby before she met him. Or she could be afraid of the reaction from any other children she has. Or perhaps her parents are elderly and ill and live with her. Maybe they're devout Catholics, and finding out that they have an illegitimate grandchild could literally kill them. You just don't know."

"No, I don't know," Shannon said. "And that's what hurts. I will probably never know."

"Shannon," Lil said. "I understand how upset you are. But you do have two parents who love you very much. Perhaps they're not biological parents, but they'd move the earth to make you happy, even if they hate your toe ring. And that's such a blessing…a blessing that many people don't have in their lives."

Shannon nodded. Lil's parents had died young; her father on his second tour in Vietnam and her mother of a rare blood disorder. Lil's paternal grandmother had raised her, and Lil had always felt somewhat odd that she didn't have a normal family.

"You're right. And I do love my mom and dad. I need to go see them and tell them that…that we can move beyond this. Tell them that in spite of the fact that we don't always see things the same way, I do adore them and am grateful for everything they've given me—"

Jane, who was facing the television in the bar, suddenly pointed. "Look! Look, it's Hal. On the news!"

Shannon whirled, spilling her drink.

A local TV newscaster asked Hal, "How do you feel, Mr. Underwood, knowing that your competitor, Greer Conover of Conover, Inc., has allegedly been engaged in corporate espionage and theft?"

She heard Hal's voice as the cameras flashed to an office building. A man was being led out the front door in handcuffs.

"Well, mostly I feel relieved to have gotten to the bottom of things. I had known we had an information leak for some time, but I hadn't pinpointed exactly how it was occurring."

"Did it come as a shock to know your own receptionist was aiding and abetting your competitor?"

The camera flashed to a still photograph of Tina.

"What?" Shannon couldn't believe her ears.

"Absolutely, it came as a shock."

"Your receptionist, Tina Wimple, claims that she was coerced and blackmailed into her actions. Do you find that claim credible?"

"I really can't comment on that at this time."

"Mr. Underwood, will this situation affect your planned IPO?"

"We will delay the IPO for a month or so, until I have all the facts in front of me, but I can assure you that our technology is still unmatched..."

"Oh. My. God." Shannon stared at her friends. "I guess he was so good in bed she confessed." She wrinkled her nose.

"Or," Jane said, "he's telling the truth and he didn't sleep with her. Didn't you say you were listening in on the date? To give him help if he ran into trouble?"

"Yeah."

"Then he was wearing a wire. You said she came

on to him first. What if she tried to strip him, found the wire and assumed he was working with the police?"

Shannon had to admit that this was a possibility.

Lilia nodded. "Drink up, Miss Shane. I think it's time you opened that envelope he dropped off."

THEY ALL DROVE back to the Finesse offices, and Shannon retrieved the envelope from her credenza. She slit it open with a pair of scissors and pulled out the contents: yet another sealed envelope and a single sheet of paper from Hal.

Dear Shannon,

Please find enclosed information on your biological parents. Don't even ask me how I came by this knowledge, but I thought you might like to have it. A private detective could possibly have found it for you, but the process would have taken much longer.

Shannon, I wish you all the best in your life. May you one day realize what a beautiful woman you are—inside. May you discover that you are a success in every sense of the word: that you are brave and talented and creative. I'd give anything to present you with that role of national prominence that you so deserve.

Since I can't do that, let me just say that you have played a very important part, however brief, in my life. I love you, Shannon. Yes, even though you've tormented me, stolen my favorite pants and charged me for the pleasure. Even though you've accused me of lying to you.

I'm absolutely positive that it's beyond un-cool for me to pour out my heart this way, but just picture me wearing shades and sitting astride a Harley as I do it.

You'll always be on the silver screen in my heart.

Love, Hal

Shannon swallowed hard and handed the letter to Jane and Lil. She fingered the sealed envelope, her palms sweating.

I hope you can feel my love from afar, for the cir-cumstances of my life do not permit me to meet you.

Her birth mother had asked her to respect her privacy.

Yet in her hands she held the answers to her past, courtesy of Hal, sweet Hal. He'd obtained the infor-mation illegally, there was no doubt about it. He must have hacked into private, secret files—she had no idea how. He'd risked his reputation and possibly his freedom for her.

And he hadn't lied to her, after all. She believed him, now.

Her hands trembling, she stuffed the envelope deep into her handbag and shoved her hands into her pockets.

"You're not going to open it?" Lil asked, incred-ulously.

"I don't know."

A wise little smile played around Jane's lips. She said nothing for a long moment, then, "Go get him, girl."

"Yeah. I'm going to try. I'm not sure I deserve him. But first, I have a phone call to make."

As her partners filed out of her office, Shannon punched in the telephone number she'd known by heart since she was six.

"Hello, Mom?"

"Shannon!" Relief and love poured down the line, even through Rebecca Shane's formal, continental accent. "I've been so worried about you. Are you all right?"

Shan nodded slowly, feeling ashamed that she'd refused to see or talk to her parents for the past few weeks.

Not lying this time, she said, "I'm fine. Mom, I just called…to tell you that I love you. I love you and Dad very much."

A swift intake of breath told her that her words had healed a wound. Her mother began to cry, elegance taking a backseat to emotion. "Oh, sweetheart. We love you, too. You are more precious to us than anything, do you hear? I haven't been a perfect mother…and your father knows he could have been around more, but—" Her voice broke. "We never meant to lie to you. We just didn't know how to bring it up. We've been cowards, and I—"

"Mom. It's okay." Though it had started out of her mouth as an automatic response, Shannon sat down on the edge of her desk, hard—because the truth of the statement overwhelmed her. She was okay. She had no identity crisis. As Hal had told her, she was herself, no matter what.

Something else occurred to her: for the first time since hearing the news that she was adopted, she realized that she wasn't the only one who needed comfort. Her mother needed reassurance, too.

She did her best to extend it, as Rebecca sobbed quietly on the other end of the line. "Mom, I've been so lucky to have you. You and Dad are my parents, no matter who actually gave birth to me. Nothing can ever change that. And Mom, I wouldn't want to."

24

SHANNON THOUGHT she'd have more time to prepare herself before seeing Hal, but he was getting out of the Explorer just as she pulled into the parking lot of his building. She hit the brakes and looked at him for a long moment. He looked back, lowering his shades à la movie star to check her out.

There were dark circles under his blue eyes and he'd managed to do something screwy to his hair. He needed another cut. Enrique would have a coronary when he saw him. Shannon didn't care a bit. To her, Hal was the model of a *GQ* guy: Genuine Quality. Gorgeously Quirky. Gallant and Quiet.

"Hi," he said, pushing the sunglasses back into place. He folded his arms across his chest. Defensive body language. He didn't want to be vulnerable to her. She bit her lip.

Then she eased her foot down on the gas pedal and pulled into the empty spot beside him. "Hi." She put the brake on. "So. Do you know of a car wash place that specializes in getting the mold out of crazy women's carpets? Because this car really stinks."

He leaned back against the door of the Explorer and looked at her through his shades, so cool that it hurt. "I might."

"Would you be willing to take a ride with the insane and show me where the place is?"

"I might."

She looked at him uncertainly. "What's my next step, here? Do I have to beg?"

He ran his tongue over his teeth and grinned wickedly. "Did I just hear that correctly? Shannon Shane, Nerd Buster, is asking *me* for guidance?"

She nodded.

"Regarding this begging," he mused. "It might be damn good for you. Would it take place, say, on your knees in front of me?"

"Is your fly zipped or unzipped in this scenario?"

He laughed and opened her passenger-side door, sliding in. "Phew. You ever heard of a product called Lysol? Take a right out of the parking lot."

She did, her mind racing as they drove. What to say to him? How to say it? Once again, she didn't know her lines. She was utterly tongue-tied. She followed his directions in silence, her cheeks warming under his amused scrutiny.

Finally they pulled into the car wash, and she rushed and bumbled to get something out before the attendants approached them. "Hal, thank you—thank you for the envelope. I mean, what was inside it. I mean, um, oh, hell. Did you do something illegal?"

His eyes inscrutable behind the shades, he remained silent and stony-faced. *Clint Eastwood, eat your heart out. This is one cool dude. A rebel—for my cause.*

Is there anything more romantic? More sexy?

Finally his lips twitched. "If I tell you, then I'll have to kill you."

"No, really. Are you, like, a criminal?"

His smile got wider, displaying a lot of gleaming white teeth. Why had she ever thought he needed whitening strips?

"Why? Does that turn you on?"

Her cheeks got hotter and she let out an embarrassed laugh.

He leaned toward her. "Then, yes. I'm a dangerous renegade. I'm wild and untamable. Only one individual can control me..." He grabbed her arm and she jumped. "My woman."

She grinned. "Really?"

"Yep."

The attendant got to them and asked what she wanted. "Oh," she said vaguely, "a car wash. And then I'll need the carpets shampooed." She couldn't look away from her newfound sexy felon.

"Pull up over there, ma'am."

She nodded.

"Punch the green button when you're ready."

"Okay." She tore her gaze away from Hal and moved the car into position. Then she took his hand. She had to get this out. "I'm so sorry that I thought you'd lied to me. You didn't, did you? I saw the news."

"No, I didn't lie. I was trying to get myself disentangled from Tina, but I guess the sound effects on your end must have been disturbing."

"I went crazy," she admitted.

"So you were jealous?"

"Out of my mind jealous."

"That's not very cool."

"No, it's not, is it?"

"Especially when you had told me to move on and see other people."

"I said that for your own good. I didn't want you to become fixated on me…it's happened to me in the past for all the wrong reasons."

"I'm not fixated on your looks, Shan. One day you'll be wrinkled and humpbacked and saggy with all the rest of us. I'll still love you because of your personality and your sense of humor and that funny thing you do with your mouth when you get embarrassed about compliments like this."

"Humpbacked?" she asked, with distaste.

"Yup. You'll be my little Quasimodo. And I'll have nose and ear hair, plus wattles like a turkey. But we'll have the most fantastic senior sex for miles around."

She started to laugh.

"We'll knock out each other's false teeth. We'll fall off the bed and not be able to get up. We'll invent a whole new position called The Walker."

"Stop it," she gasped. When she recovered, she said, "I love you."

"What?"

"I love you." She took a deep breath. "I do. I think I've loved you since you answered to the name 'Saddam' and sprung a woody in my visitor's chair."

He cringed. "You noticed that?"

"Sorry. It was like the Washington Monument. It was unavoidable."

"Thank you. I think." He leaned over and kissed her, long and hard. His stubble scraped her face as he pulled away. "There is only one thing that stops me from indecently proposing to you right this minute."

"Really?" She was delighted. Then she frowned. "Is it because I'm a little wacky?"

"No." His expression turned serious, and her heart sank.

"Is it because you're already married?"

He shook his head. "No, that's not it."

She'd been kidding, but she exhaled in relief anyway. "Is it because we've only known each other about three weeks?"

Hal took her chin in his hand. "Yeah, that's partly it. We should wait at least four. But the main reason is that I want my damn pants back!"

She threw her arms wide, accidentally hitting the green car-wash button. "Oh, is that all? I have— Oh, *shit!* The top's down!"

But it was too late. She'd parked in correct position, and they were pulled forward by the mechanized car wash.

"Duck," Hal yelled.

Blue and white rotating foam straps whirred down on them, beating them and dumping cold, soapy water everywhere. They hunched over and just prayed for it to be over soon. They went through another beating with the second wash cycle and then finally endured the rinse.

Approximately five minutes later, they emerged on the other side. Hal stared at the vehicular lake they were now riding in, tried to glare at her, but broke down laughing. "When you asked me to take a ride with the insane, I had no idea."

Shannon shifted against her drenched seat and winced. "Uh, sorry?" She pushed her wet hair out of her face and wrung it out.

"You have destroyed this car. The only thing you're fit to drive is an army-issue jeep, and I'm not sure I'd trust you with that. I don't know that I'd even give you a Big Wheel."

She ignored these comments. "As I was saying," she informed him, "I have your pants in the trunk."

"The Dumpster pants?"

"Well, no. But one of the original pairs that came out of your closet. I bought them back from Goodwill."

He wiped his face with the back of his hand and squinted at her. "You gonna charge me for them?"

"Only a very modest handling fee—*aaaiiieeeee!*" He tackled her and tickled. "Stop it!" She shrieked. "Stop! Okay, okay, they're free! I was kidding…."

Breathless, she collapsed against the wet seat and

surveyed the car again. "Well, at least it was already moldy in here. That's something."

"You're something. Something else!" Hal kissed her again, and they fell into a wet, tangled heap while several car-wash attendants looked on curiously and elbowed each other in the ribs.

When he raised his head, he said, "Do you, crazy Shannon, take me, Hal, to be your awfully wetted boyfriend?"

She traced his jaw with her fingers and looked into his impossibly blue eyes. She'd never loved any man like she loved Hal. He'd turned her inside out...and liked her even better that way.

"Well, of course I do. Now shut up and kiss me."

* * * * *

Don't miss Lilia's story. Watch for
OPEN INVITATION?
Coming In October 2005
from Harlequin Blaze.

THE SECRET DIARY

**A new drama unfolds for six
of the state's wealthiest bachelors.**

This newest installment continues with

ROUND-THE-CLOCK TEMPTATION
by Michelle Celmer

(Silhouette Desire, #1683)

When Nita Windcroft is assigned a bodyguard,
she's determined to refuse. She needs an
investigator, not a protector. But one look
at Connor Thorne—a quiet challenge begging
to be solved—and she realizes that having him
around all the time is a sensual opportunity
she can't resist!

*Available October 2005
at your favorite retail outlet.*

If you enjoyed what you just read,
then we've got an offer you can't resist!

Take 2 bestselling
love stories FREE!
Plus get a FREE surprise gift!

Clip this page and mail it to Harlequin Reader Service®

IN U.S.A.	IN CANADA
3010 Walden Ave.	P.O. Box 609
P.O. Box 1867	Fort Erie, Ontario
Buffalo, N.Y. 14240-1867	L2A 5X3

YES! Please send me 2 free Harlequin® Blaze™ novels and my free surprise gift. After receiving them, if I don't wish to receive anymore, I can return the shipping statement marked cancel. If I don't cancel, I will receive 6 brand-new novels each month, before they're available in stores! In the U.S.A., bill me at the bargain price of $3.99 plus 25¢ shipping and handling per book and applicable sales tax, if any*. In Canada, bill me at the bargain price of $4.47 plus 25¢ shipping and handling per book and applicable taxes**. That's the complete price and a savings of at least 10% off the cover prices—what a great deal! I understand that accepting the 2 free books and gift places me under no obligation ever to buy any books. I can always return a shipment and cancel at any time. Even if I never buy another book from Harlequin, the 2 free books and gift are mine to keep forever.

151 HDN D7ZZ
351 HDN D72D

Name	(PLEASE PRINT)	
Address	Apt.#	
City	State/Prov.	Zip/Postal Code

Not valid to current Harlequin® Blaze™ subscribers.

Want to try two free books from another series?
Call 1-800-873-8635 or visit www.morefreebooks.com.

* Terms and prices subject to change without notice. Sales tax applicable in N.Y.
** Canadian residents will be charged applicable provincial taxes and GST.
  All orders subject to approval. Offer limited to one per household.
  ® and ™ are registered trademarks owned and used by the trademark owner and/or its licensee.

BLZ05   ©2005 Harlequin Enterprises Limited.

Available this October from

DANGER BECOMES YOU

(Silhouette Desire #1682)

by Annette Broadrick

Another compelling story featuring

Brothers bound by blood
and the land they love.

Jase Crenshaw was desperate for
solitude, so imagine his shock when his
secluded mountain cabin was invaded
by a woman just as desperate—but only
Jase could provide help.

Available wherever Silhouette Books are sold.

COMING NEXT MONTH

#207 OPEN INVITATION? Karen Kendall
The Man-Handlers, Bk. 3

He's a little rough around the edges. In fact, Lilia London has no idea how to polish Dan Granger. With only a few weeks to work, she has no time to indulge the steamy attraction between them. But he's so sexy when he's persistent. Maybe she'll indulge… just a little.

#208 FAKING IT Dorie Graham
Sexual Healing, Bk. 3

What kind of gift makes men sick? Erin McClellan doesn't have the family talent for sexual healing. So she's sworn off guys…until she meets the tempting Jack Langston. When he's still strong the next morning, she wants to hit those sheets one more time!

#209 PRIVATE RELATIONS Nancy Warren
Do Not Disturb

PR director Kit Prescott is throwing a Fantasy Weekend Contest to promote Hush—Manhattan's hottest boutique hotel. The first winner is sexy, single—and her ex-fiancé, Peter Garson! How can Kit entertain the man who's never stopped starring in all *her* fantasies?

#210 TALKING ABOUT SEX… Vicki Lewis Thompson

Engineer Jess Harkins has always had a thing for Katie Peterson. He could even have been her first lover…if he'd had the nerve to take her up on her offer. Now Katie's an opinionated shock jock who obviously hasn't forgiven him, given the way she's killing his latest project over the airwaves. So what can Jess do but teach her to put her mouth to better use?

#211 CAN'T GET ENOUGH Sarah Mayberry

Being stuck in an elevator can do strange things to people. And Claire Marsden should know. The hours she spent with archrival Jack Brook resulted in the hottest sex she's ever had! She'd love to forget the whole thing…if only she didn't want to do it again.

#212 POSSESSION Tori Carrington
Dangerous Liaisons, Bk. 1

When FBI agent Akela Brooks returns home to New Orleans, she never expects to end up as a hostage of Claude Lafitte, the accused Quarter killer—or to enjoy her captivity so much. She immediately knows the sexy Cajun is innocent of murder. But for Akela, that doesn't make him any less dangerous.…

www.eHarlequin.com

HBCNM0905